ISBN **978-0-9856291-0-6**

Book 2 of a series with these characters, the 1st in the series entitled Empty Man.

This book is dedicated to my wife and my friends
that for some unfathomable reason put up with me.

4

Cry Havoc

William Shakespeare's Julius Caesar; Act III Scene one.

ANTONY: Blood and destruction shall be so in use And dreadful objects so familiar That mothers shall but smile when they behold Their infants quarter'd with the hands of war; All pity choked with custom of fell deeds: And Caesar's spirit, ranging for revenge, With Ate by his side come hot from hell, Shall in these confines with a monarch's voice Cry "Havoc," and let slip the dogs of war; That this foul deed shall smell above the earth With carrion men, groaning for burial.

6

Cry Havoc

Preface

Stapled to his basement walls were giant Sponge Bob caricatures in full cartoon color. Toys were stashed carefully, if not neatly, in the corner of the room. Several discrete HD cameras had been placed around the room from various angles all hooked to his monster Mac desktop array, which would be considered suitable for HD and even 3D film production. The productions he created, at least the ones created in this room, seldom received any acclaim. In fact, they were seldom seen outside of a few exclusive residential theaters. Never intended for mainstream viewing, these were guarded and hidden, even destroyed when anyone discovered the mere possibility of their existence.

The truth is that his profits merely paid for his passion, which had nothing to do with the kiddy porn or with his exclusive and discreet crew and talent. He even reviled the ones that bought his "work" for sexual gratification. But he sold them anyway. Personally, he preferred the fear in their eyes. Better still, the abject terror in a small child's eyes when the child realizes that despite what momma said, there really are monsters.

8

Chapter 1

Malibu is one of those places where, "what you see is what you get." If you expected the denizens of this bastion of wealth on the coast of California to be petty and shallow, you would be mostly right. There are, in the alternative, such places as the Sierra Retreat, run by a group of Franciscan monks who have taken a vow of poverty. Even though, Malibu is generally not an area of high crime. The crime rate for Malibu in 2009 was lower than the national average across the board. Violent crimes were lower by 55.42% and the property crime rate by 29.12%. Against comparable numbers in the rest of the state of California, average violent crime rate in Malibu was lower by 59.44%.

In a different basement workshop altogether, now memorialized in FBI lore but never actually visited by an active FBI agent, even has a plaque on the wall, expressing the thanks of a grateful nation for his assistance in stopping an international terrorist. The one FBI agent who had been in Justin's basement had retired the day before and was fully aware that the vile "terrorist" was not actually dead, but was now a full-time Deputy Sheriff in Rankin County Mississippi. A humorous turn of circumstances. It seems that the terrorist was actually just a vengeful husband and father, doing what most of us would do.

The plaque was for two deeds which Justin is still able to laugh about in extremely private and discreet company. First for pointing out the flaws in the FBI's brand new computer setup and second for plugging all of the holes in their "state of the art" system.

The joke being that he provided them with only enough information to shield him and his coconspirators from prosecution in the death of the vile terrorist, and further that the "plug" allowed him unfettered access to their system. Even if they did see him snooping, he would send them a bill saying it was for maintenance and they would gratefully pay.

The picture frozen on his computer screen is the picture of what used to be an innocent young child. Past tense, not because the child is dead, but because the innocence was irreparably torn from the child's heart and mind, leaving an unfixable hole. A damaged soul.

Despite Justin's soft outward appearance, he hadn't shed a tear for years, until he saw the look of defeat and resignation in the eye of the young child on the screen. He dials the sender of the picture. He waits anxiously until the voice on the other end says, "Haywood Investigations. Haywood speaking."

"You confuse me, Haywood. What the hell are you

sending me this vile shit for?"

"I thought maybe you guys needed a "cause célèbre" to have something to get pissed off about." Silence on the phone. "Well?"

"OK, I'm pissed."

Haywood sends some more information with a click on his computer and says, "That's everything we know about who ever is putting this stuff out. I was hoping that, well since he's evidently a big computer guy, that maybe you guys would be interested in putting him out of business." Haywood hears nothing from the other end, so asks, "You there?"

"Yeah, yeah, I'm thinking."

"There have been rumors about some guy with computer skills putting out kiddy porn, torture and even kiddy snuff films to a very elite clientele. This is the first one we have actually seen. The guy that had this copy died of a massive heart attack, and this was the last thing he saw on his computer screen."

"There is a God. Anybody that touches this should have their dick nibbled off by a heard of rats. Massive heart attack is too quick."

"You're in then?"

"Let me call the guys, but yeah, we're in."

"Can you find him?"

Justin thinks about it for a few seconds and then

responds. "We may have to go back on our promise about weapons, but yeah we'll find him."

Haywood smiles knowing he has just recruited the least likely conglomeration of allies that he had ever personally grown to love. "You say "Hi" to the boys for me then."

As they click off, Haywood says coldly, "Cry Havoc, and let slip the dogs of war."

Chapter 2

The eight that Justin had intended to gather in the impeccably furnished living room of this lovely Malibu home, were an odd grouping of 8 totally different personalities consisting entirely of four husbands and their wives. which originally would have been described as four wives and their husbands. The distinction is because the four wives have known each other since college. The wives consisting of one noted surgeon, one successful Real Estate Agent, and two other professional women, that dragged their wealthy and well educated husbands, kicking and screaming to function after function, brunch after cheese and wine tasting with the other husbands. The four men on the surface seem so different that they would never be able to bond. This being a point of fact, for which the four wives still feel a smidgen of guilt.

Despite the differences they did bond. The largest, Albert Finney would appear more comfortable in a wrestling ring or climbing the side of the Empire State Building. Albert is a 45-year-old, retired "All Pro" Linebacker. A very large man, even in a sport filled with very large men. Again, Malibu being Malibu, with the rapid influx of rappers, recording industry moguls, among others, the only reason anyone would stare at a black man would be to determine if he was a celebrity. Albert was a soft-spoken and articulate graduate of Northwestern University. He was famous only on the football field and only with his helmet on. As such he may have been a household name, but hardly a recognizable face. He is in Malibu because he worships his beautiful and talented wife Barbara. Barbara is an orthopedic surgeon at the Ronald Reagan Medical Center at UCLA. They met immediately after his career ended with two minutes left in the fourth quarter of a huge playoff game in San Diego. Airlifted to UCLA for treatment, he became enamored with his surgeon. After being rebuked and refused repeatedly by her, telling him frequently that besides the doctor patient "thing', she vehemently hated football and football players with every fiber of her body. Even so, for some bizarre reason, she decided to give him a chance. Albert is part of the group because he is retired, bored and craves action.

If there is an opposite to Albert, Justin Cummings would be it. He is an overweight 35-year-old, with a pasty complexion and the mandatory frizzy red hair. If being a nerd were a crime, his picture would be at the post office, instead of the cover of "Wired" magazine (twice). Last year when he sold his "Dot Com" for a price he is embarrassed to discuss in public, he was given the choice either to go to work for them (not friggin likely) or to agree not to compete.

So he signed a "non-competition" agreement. The terms were so strict, unalterable, inescapable and unbreakable that their lawyer joked that if he flushed a toilet, it would probably be a minor violation. At the time, it seemed like a good idea. Remarkably, he is married and truly cherished (to everyone's amazement) by his wife Evelyn, currently seated next to him. She is the sister of Mrs. Barbara Finney. Albert's spouse. To Evelyn, Justin is somehow, mysteriously perfect. To most people, he's just a goofball.

The next coconspirator is Evander De La Silva, 52 years old, with thick dark hair and cleft chin, movie star good looks and a movie star's wardrobe. He represents old money from Montecito, California. Montecito is an oasis of vast wealth 10 minutes south of downtown Santa Barbara and one hour and a hiccup up the coast from Malibu on PCH. His reputation, well earned, is that he has never worked nor given a shit about anything (at all). In truth he has started many jobs, but, as the sole heir to his family's vast fortune, he does not need to work, so he simply has chosen not to, a choice that left him searching for some meaning to his life. A lifelong philanderer and lover of women, Evan surprisingly found his match. Although none of his family or friends believed that the marriage would last a week, it has lasted a full 16 years. The next member of the group is, his wife, Cherry De La Silva. she is an undergraduate classmate of Barbara's and close friend of Evelyn's.

The last of the group's core members is Robert Anderson, a handsome and rugged-looking 61-year-old, with a slight Napoleon complex, who tells anyone that asks that he is a retired businessman, which is technically accurate though he refuses to act like one. After the Army in Viet Nam, he went to school on the GI bill and learned he had a knack for determining the value of large businesses. He married the boss's daughter at Johnston Dickens, the fourth largest pharmaceutical company in the world. After being forced out for a pittance by his father in law when his bored, spoiled wife left him for a tennis pro, he shorted the company stock and then dumped a number of files in the media toilet. The files contained multiple references about skipped mandatory steps during drug testing (all true).

He then came west and married the love of his life, a noted realtor from Malibu. Together they bought a huge house on the beach and settled in. In the peace and tranquillity of Malibu however, he is bored out of his mind. The last of the eight members of this conglomeration, his wife Mary, is a lovely and gifted woman who also happens to be the best friend and confidant of Evelyn, Barbara and Cherry.

This time, the meeting consists of all four coconspirators and two wives. A multitude of reasons for the grouping, all completely agreed to by all parties as a direct result of the latest series of misadventures. The wives' participation in the group came at a steep price from each side; The wives taking a total vow of secrecy and the husbands taking a vow that some things were off limits. The truth is, that even Barbara, the staunchest pacifist, had to acknowledge that she was proud of what they had accomplished, although she still smoldered about some of the tactics and some of the chances they had employed. The concluding element in favor of the husbands being able to consider future quests was that Special Agent Samuel Haywood Retired had made the four vow to not use weapons of any kind, and to avoid direct contact at all costs, with out a consensus from the entire group.

Barbara was committed to surgery this morning. So she had insisted that at least two of the four wives be present to hear about any "adventure" before they would vote to endorse it.

From the wive's perspective, fully realizing that their husbands would do whatever they wanted in the end, it meant the wives would only have a limited tactical control over the "jobs" their husbands would take on. From the husbands' perspective, they counted on their wives to keep them from the really stupid things they might do to battle boredom. Yes, the four men were together because they were all bored -- Like robbing banks and blowing stuff up. Together, the eight were capable of doing some actual good.

Explaining that even to have this "garbage" on their computer was a federal crime, Justin showed the group the video. He intentionally left out parts involving actual sexual acts against the frail child. The point had been made, there wasn't a dry eye in the room. Justin had converted the entire sequence to digital so he could evaluate and research it, but it could not now be saved or reproduced in any form which could ever be seen again.

"I will dedicate whatever time it takes to find out how to stop whoever is doing this," Justin vows.

Albert shakes his head and says, "I'm not sure what I will do, but I know it'll involve a meat thermometer, an electrical outlet and some jumper cables."

Cherry, Evan's wife, is wiping her eyes and asks, "This is against the law. Why not turn it over to the police?"

Justin responds, "That's who we got it from, or at least from Haywood. He knows that they don't have the ability to find them, and if we find them, they can't use the information in court, so it's a waist of time. If you want, we could ask a lawyer?"

Robert spits out, "What are we going to learn from a lawyer?"

Justin answers, "What we can give to the cops that they can use. Basically, how far we need to go to actually do any good. Without putting ourselves in harms way, or messing up a conviction."

Evelyn adds, "Or being sued or going to jail."

Robert disgusted adds, "I hate lawyers. All of them."

Albert remembering Robert's massive reasons for his hatred, stifles a laugh and slaps Robert on the back. "Your problem was not the lawyers, it was your father in law."

Robert retorts, "Yeah and the lawyers made a bad situation worse."

Justin answers, "Robert, you ended up free and clear with a pot full of money, your father in law is broke and in prison!"

Evan adds, "And your ex wife is living with a relative since the tennis pro dumped her when he found out she was broke!"

Robert smiles meekly, "You guys are just trying to cheer me up." They all laugh.

Justin knocks on the table, "We need to vote here. Ladies first."

The four look to Justin's wife Evelyn and Evan's wife Cherry to begin the vote. Evelyn starts, "It's every woman's dream to have their children safe form harm. Since none of us have children of our own, it seems fair that we still need to find a way to do what we can to make children safe."

Cherry asks, "But what can we do?"

They look at Justin who shrugs and responds, "We can find 'em. Then use "em as bait to move up the food chain or turn em over to the cops. We can burn their eyes out with hot pokers,... I guess that one may get voted down."

He looks at his wife who reaches over and touches her husband's face with her fingertips. Evelyn says, "Justin has a soft spot."

Evan interjects, "In his head," drawing a chuckle.

Evelyn continues, "In his "heart" for children. He has already vented to me on this and left all of the implements of torture back at our house."

Robert holds up his hand palm forward and turns to crack a joke, "Too much information, consenting adults and all. Look, whatever you guys are into at home." Cherry and Evelyn's eyes together freeze to smile off Robert's face. "OK, I know."

Cherry adds, "We'll tell Barbara that we're in. All the way in as long as it's just pedophiles and not gun play."

Evan says, "Then it's unanimous as far as I can see it."

Chapter 3

Justin, back in his man cave, computers purring away while he's tinkering with a new electronic toy. After researching the problem on the FBI computer, he is surprised that so little information is available on kiddy porn combined with kiddy snuff films. Suddenly one of his monitors beeps with an old-fashioned bell sound effect. Justin looks up and reads a note on the screen, "Bingo." He sets down his newest gizmo and dials his cell phone. After a moment, he says, "Got him!"

Every day except on Saturday and Sunday the local Malibu sports bar offers two things, a very good selection of beers, ales and brews, kept a fraction of a degree above freezing, and privacy. Although huge with young boys and girls in Malibu, soccer has yet to catch on among adult men. So there is really no other reason to go to a sports bar after baseball season, at least during the week. On Tuesdays, the four had a regular spot in the far corner of the bar again for several reasons. It's a big booth (Albert being a large man) and the view of the bank of televisions is least visible from this booth. These four "un-American" Americans simply don't watch sports on Television. Robert, the last to walk in, winks at the bartender and orders a brew on the way to the corner and bows to the group, "Sorry, Mary wants me to take a real estate test and I was reading some stuff for the test. I think it's crap. Can you picture me sitting in some open house for 4 hours smiling and shaking hands? I don't think so!"

Justin perks up, "No, do it, the real estate software is trick. You get access to all kinds of property information."

Evan asks, "Don't you already have access to that stuff?"

"Well yeah, but I have to do it illegally. Why not break into the mainstream?"

Albert buts in, "You have the address, lets go take a look."

"Well, for that, I got an IP address."

Evan, quizzically, "Is this a sophomoric joke like I P Freely?"

Justin who is sometimes perturbed by jokes about what he has determined about basic knowledge, sips his beer and gets "that look'. so Albert starts, "No, no ,no you don't. Justin, You are talking to guys who love you, dude. The fact that at least one of us is dumber than a sack of rocks means you need to explain some stuff, that's all."

Justin leans forward and starts, "Everything attached to the Internet is assigned an I.P. number, short for "Internet Protocol'. After like a gazillon things have been hooked up to the Internet, including like every other cell phone, there are too many, so they issued them to "host servers'. So, since these numbers are usually assigned to Internet service providers within region-based blocks, an IP address can be used to identify a region which a computer is connecting to the Internet. An IP address can show the user's general location. Some country rules are strict and some aren't, so if you go through certain countries, you consider yourself protected and through others you have very little expectation of privacy."

"Boring." Says Evan. When everyone turns to look at him, he adds, "Sorry. Please continue."

"OK yeah it's boring, I get it. But this IP address went through a specialized server in Sierra Leone. Which is stupid on so many levels that it's brilliant. When people think of Sierra Leone, they think things like conflicts diamonds, Civil War and poverty, not the Internet. So in general we think of the Internet there like two cans tied together with string. We disregard it totally. The bad news for them is that the security measures are nonexistent so I can swoop in and find out who is doing what to who."

Robert interrupts, "Whom." but is stared down by both Albert and Evan. "Sorry."

Albert scolds jokingly, "Children."

Justin gets the point, however. "The point--" Evan and Robert applaud as Albert glares at both of them. "The original sender came from a host right down the street."

Silence. So he continues, "Not impressed yet? OK, it's a cheesy Internet cafe. So I did a backtrack to find out who had sent anything to Sierra Leone, and one account came up. A bad name, but a good credit card. Issued to a Metro Goldwyn Mayer account that was supposed to be closed a decade ago to a guy who retired and died a week later."

Evan asks, "And this helps us how?"

Justin unfolds a piece of paper an sets it on the table.

The address is within 2 blocks of Evan's house on the PCH in Malibu. "This is him." He cues his smart phone and a video starts. A heavyset man walks out of a Starbucks off Cross Creek Rd at PCH.

Robert notices, "Hey that's right over there by the theater."

Albert asks, "That fat guy? He must go three bills."

Evan jokes, "Shit, we can track him from space."

Chapter 4

Cars in Malibu fall into three basic classifications: classic cars, luxury cars and invisible. In a place where the "invisible" category are completely ignored, the 1980 Ford van replete with ladder and broken (but duck -taped) side mirror is invisible. Not even a punch line in a bad joke.

Purchased and repaired in loving memory of a previous such white van, this one was the very best running, ugly beat-up and tired looking vehicle you could imagine. Justin, at the wheel, turns into the Starbucks and parks at the Cross Creek side parking area which is only four cars wide. After the morning rush hour, the Starbucks area parking is mostly empty. Justin slips into the parking position at the end, closest to the edge of Starbucks. Robert, in the back, asks, "He always parks here?"

"Usually," responds Justin as he puts the van in park, turns off the ignition and says, "I don't want this to be a pooch screw here, so if there is a surprise, we come back tomorrow. He comes here every day at the same time, so we can take our time. Today, tomorrow, next week."

Albert starts, "OK you be in the Starbucks texting as lookout. When he comes out, you want me to walk right past here," pointing at the sidewalk directly in front of the van.

Justin responds, "Wait until he's almost at the corner, then walk casually past."

Albert shakes his head, "And he's going to cut between the van and whatever car is next to it just to avoid walking next to me?"

Robert Perks up, holds up his hand and says, "I would. You don't look like a football player, you look like a small building." Evan nods agreement.

Albert raises his head and says, "You assholes. That's some raciest shit."

Evan retorts "And not the first time it worked in your favor."

Robert corrects, "Albert, the truth is it would work exactly the same if you were white."

Justin nods, "Yup. He's a coward, not a racist. I see you walking and I don't know you, I do the same. OK?" Albert nods. Justin continues "Back to work. Just like what Uri, I mean Leo did, Robert ties his shoe and forces him to walk between him and the van."

Robert adds, "So I just I taze him and roll him into the van, simple."

Albert shakes his head disagreeing, "The dude weighs over thee hundred pounds. He goes to the ground and there will be a scene."

Justin replies, "We do what Leo did. You hit him on the

neck and then just," Justin makes circular motions with his hands, "You know, push him into the van using his own momentum.

Robert interrupts, "If he cooperates. If he doesn't, then we play it by ear. Once he's in the van, Evan takes his car keys and drives Justin to his house to get computer stuff. Then everything goes to the "Trailer" and we decide the next step."

In position, a black AMC Mercedes 500 "S" pulls up and parks at the opposite end of the four-space parking area and the target, Lloyd Archibald Weber, rose to his full five-foot eight-inch, 320-pound height and ambled into the coffee shop. Supporting a well-quaffed head of wavy dark brown hair and blemish-free face, he was actually better looking than the four had expected. Well dressed in clothing tailored to his physique, Lloyd was fashionable. Justin texts to Albert, "His car is here, is he on his way?" Just as Lloyd turned the corner, Justin texts, "Never mind. I see him." Justin then switches to a different open program and slides his mouse pad slightly rotating a traffic camera at the corner away from the Starbucks parking area.

The clerks confer when they see Lloyd through the window and although one is too quiet to be heard, the other responds, "Cheap asshole, spit in his coffee." The door dings and the same clerk says, "Good morning Sir, good to see you again, sir."

Lloyd snarls in his "Elvis" lip pout and saunters up to the empty line and orders, "The regular!"

The clerk confirms, "Non-fat caramel latte, decaf soy milk, grande?"

Lloyd nods, annoyed and clearly above any useless and pointless conversation with a mere mortal. Justin rolls his eyes.

Lloyd drops a $5 bill on the counter, takes his change and slips a nickel into the tip jar, and both clerks say, "Thank you, bye." As Lloyd walks out the door, one adds, "Asshole." as the door closes.

Justin who had never stopped texting a blow by blow of the visit, closes his laptop, slides a $10 bill into the tip jar and walks the opposite direction through the opposite side door and around the corner to the group.

In back of the Starbucks, on cue, Albert walks the sidewalk but instead of cutting between the van and the next car, Lloyd sees Albert and goes completely around the van to avoid him. Robert moves the few feet and opens the rear doors of the van, looking around and seeing nobody paying any attention as Lloyd comes around the back of the van. Lloyd stops for a second and Robert ask him, "Did you really just tip them a nickel in there?"

Lloyd, startled, asks, "What did you say?" Just then

Evan walks around behind Lloyd and sets the Taser on Lloyd's ear.

Instead of swinging him gently into the van, Lloyd slides out of their grip like 320 pounds of jello to the ground. Robert says simply, "Shit!" Surprisingly, still no one is paying any attention. Evan says, "Then you swing him gently into the van. Isn't that what Uri said?"

Albert steps around the van and says, "Pick him up, what are you waiting for?"

Together, Evan, Robert and Albert lift as much of him as they can and wiggle him into the rear of the van. Still amazed that no one seems to pay any attention, Albert hands Lloyd's keys to Evan and crawls into the back and pulls the door shut. Robert climbs in the van as Evan and Justin put on rubber gloves and climbs in Lloyd's car.

Chapter 5

At Lloyd's house, Justin calls up the blueprints on his smart phone and says pointing at a spot on his phone, "Unless he's done more changes, I'm betting what we want is right here in the basement." After entering through the garage and disabling the alarm system with the entry of the appropriate number, Evan asks as they walk through the kitchen, "OK you sneaky bastard, how'd you do that?"

Justin responds, "Evan, quiet. I just know stuff like that."

Evan thinks and says, "Then what's my secret security code?"

Justin shushes Evan and continues looking around. Evan continues, "So your fallible? Not Mr. Perfect? I'll let Robert and Albert know that, ..."

Justin interrupts whispering jokingly, "5125. 51 being your age when you set the code and 25 being your I. Q."

Evan stops in his tracks with his mouth open speechless as Justin walks to the hall closet and says, "Somewhere right here."

Evan walks up behind him and asks, "So you ever go into my house when I'm not there?"

Justing feels the door jam and then opens the closet door and feels inside while talking, "I don't have a key do I.

You ask, I will answer with the truth. If you don't really want to know, don't ask! Now be quiet." He touches something on the wall inside the closet and smiles. They both hear a very slight click and the wall inside of the closet opens into a stairwell downward. "Sweet."

Justin reaches inside and locates a light switch and they both proceed to the basement.

At the bottom of the stairs is an unfinished but completely drywalled area with two doors. Through the drywall tape it is clear that one side is about twice the size of the other side, so Justin says, "You take that side," pointing at the larger side, "and I'll take this side. Remember, pictures first."

Evan opens the door and is transported to the obscene room from the video replete with pictures on the wall and toys. His initial reaction is disgust and then a double dose of creepiness sets in as he takes a video of the room and he sees the video being shot on his iPhone and can't help but think of the children. He says barely audibly, "This was one sick pud."

A slightly processed voice comes from some invisible speaker in the room, "What?" and Evan scurries out of the room to look for Justin.

Justing was on his back on the floor checking out the video hookup feeds from under the elaborate video/audio workstation. "I said, what?"

"Shit that was you. I heard a processed voice in the other room and it freaked me a bit. That is surreal. How many children did he ruin in there?"

Justin keeps working, "From the storage rack, at least 20, but who knows. It could be the same kid. This is some exclusive gear. Like major studio gear." Justin comes out from under the desk and checks his hands, holding them up for Evan to see. "See, no dust, no dirt. He cleaned under there. I can't imagine he had a service do it." He points at a rack and says, "There are about twenty disks, that could be more or less than twenty kids, but I'm guessing one per disk."

"Sick."

"This computer is totally custom next-generation stuff. Let's run it up to the trailer and I'll check it out." He re adjusts his gloves and starts disconnecting wires and equipment. "We'll take this and this and this thing here," pointing at electronic equipment in a built-in rack mount station. "The rack looks permanent, so here's a screwdriver."

Evan is not excited about the screwdriver but takes it and starts disassembling the gear. "Can I look through his wine cellar to see if he has anything cool?"

"Don't touch anything until I check it for booby traps, but why not look?"

Evan asks, "Booby traps? Are you kidding?"

Justin starts to answer when his phone vibrates and he checks it, saying, "Robert's outside. I'll take this stuff up. And No, I'm not kidding. This shit is seriously criminal, so bombs, guns -- or whatever wouldn't surprise me at all." He grabs the bulky computer tower and exits.

Chapter 6

Ernie Alvarez, an overweight high school dropout with an aptitude for all things computer, mans a sophisticated room filled with electronics. Although it's a tedious place, Ernie considers it an upscale alarm monitoring station. Further, because he knows that he is overpaid and occasionally ask to do questionable things, he fully appreciates that not everything this room monitors is legal.

Bored by the monotony, he is currently eating a folded pizza slice, not caring the least that the sauce is dripping on the floor. One of the monitors rings with the chirp-chirp sound of some baby bird, and he lays down the pizza and picks up a napkin to wipe his hands superficially on the way to the monitor. At the monitor he sits and presses a button, then dials his cell phone, "Ernie here, we have a movement alert on the computer at the Weber location." He listens, "Yes sir, I will track and call back in one hour." He hangs up and sets the timer on his watch for one hour. "Yeah whatever, asshole." Then he walks back to folded pizza slice and sits down. His cell phone rings, and he answers it but does not recognize the voice. "Sorry, I work for, ..."

He is interrupted by an irritated male voice with a slight Russian accent saying, "Do you want me to come down there and rip your testicles off?"

Ernie stutters his response. "Ne,.. na,... no sir." He wipes his fingers on his pants and sits down in front of a monitor and places the phone down pressing the speaker button.

The voice comes through the speaker impatiently, "Where is it now?"

"About 4 miles and moving."

"South?"

"No sir, North."

"North? Get a precise GPS reading when it stops for at least 30 minutes and then call me at the number on your phone's screen now. Understand?"

He looks at the number and without asking who is calling, says, "Yes sir."

A click is heard on the speaker ending the call. "Take a chill." He stops and confirms that the line is dead, "Mr. Dramatic, Mr. Asshole. Even for $25.00 an hour I don't need this shit."

He goes back to his pizza and carries the crusty remains to the monitor and checks. "OK, you stopped you little bugger. So now we wait." He checks his watch for the time.

He sits at another computer and inserts the coordinates and a map pops up. "Nothing there. Just a, ... something. Well it's not in someone's garage at least."

Chapter 7

The "trailer" which is actually a 10-by 50-foot mobile home, is not a likely spot for the conspirators. It was shabby, especially when parked behind the lineup of luxury vehicles that the four generally drove -- today it was parked behind the Van, an Audi 8 and two near identical Mercedes AMC's, both black, both 500 S.

On the other hand, the three acres of prime ocean-view property in the hills above Malibu where the vehicles and mobile home now rested was a perfect spot to meet. The property is a quarter mile up a dirt road off PCH-- "trail" may be a better. The turnoff to the trailer is easily missed. If however you look on the other side of the street for a beat-up, rusted-out mailbox with the name "MARSHALL", then you just turn between the two largest trees opposite and find the trail. A trail because it can hardly be called a driveway.

In the back bedroom, furnished with a single unmade bed and a blacked-out window, Lloyd, the guest of honor, is bound hand and foot by jumbo-sized Tie Raps with a hood over his head and noise-canceling headphones over his ears. Albert, seated by Lloyd, Taser in his hand, watching news on a small television. "Nothing on TV. Was anyone at Lloyd's house, and ... where's Justin?"

Robert sits down and answers, "In the shed. We won't see him for a while."

The three pull Lloyd's hood and headphones off, and Lloyd's panic turns quickly to confusion. Then his eyes adjust to his surroundings and he is more confused, so he starts talking despite the leather gag between his teeth. Albert asks the other two, "Does he think we can understand him?"

Robert unties the gag and, as Lloyd attempts to get the stiffness out of his jaw, he asks Lloyd seriously, "So you never thought those parking tickets would catch up with you did you?" Evan and Albert laugh.

Lloyd looks at the three men and his surroundings, "I can get money. I promise. Let me go, I didn't do anything to you guys."

Robert catches his eye and he says calmly and clearly, "Pervert."

Lloyd is more confused but a spreading look of grave concern also starts to appear across his visage. Nervous he asks, "What are you talking about?"

Evan takes his cell phone out and shows him a brief clip of his downstairs room. Albert asks, "Was that creepy to do?"

Evan nods as the video comes to an end. "He's got

speakers and microphones and voice-altering stuff down there. Creepy is an appropriate word."

Lloyd's fluster turns to fury, and he retorts, "I know my rights, I'm a lawyer!" His attempted tirade stops abruptly when Robert swings angrily and breaks his nose. Lloyd struggles in his bonds, blood running freely down his face.

"Ouch, damn that hurt!" Robert yells as he jumps up and down and shakes his fist violently in the air. "Damn. That hurt!""

Albert wipes Lloyd's nose and says, "Don't blow. It'll make it worse. Now, do we have your attention? So what do you know about us?"

"You're not cops. You live in a shitty trailer." Then looking at Robert, Lloyd says, "He's an asshole. And you guys are criminals."

Robert steps forward and is restrained by Evan, who has his back to Lloyd and is smiling broadly and trying not to show it. Evan says to Robert, "OK, big boy. We'll let you cut off his fingers when the time comes."

Showing the first signs of fear, Lloyd asks, "Why would you cut off my fingers?"

Albert responds matter-of-factly, "So they won't be able to identify the body."

With unconvincing bravado, Lloyd blurts, "I'm hungry and I'm not going to cooperate if you don't feed me."

Evan now finally laughs out loud, "We don't want you to

cooperate, Mr. Bond. We want you to die!"

Albert shakes his head. "That's not entirely true. We want information that you may or may not possess, and you will tell us all you know or you will suffer."

Lloyd shows his confusion and looks from Albert to Robert to Evan. "I don't understand, what do you want?"

Robert leans in and leers at Lloyd saying, "I want to kill a lawyer, so I get a bonus with you."

Albert, always the calm one says, "You need to relax and consider whether you want to live and what you're willing to do for that. Oh, yell all you want, that's OK with us." Then he looks at the other two and says, "Gentlemen, lets go allow Lloyd to think." And the three leave the room.

Chapter 8

The isolated, cliff-side home was an engineering feat to be admired, not counting the amazing setting and the three-hundred-degree view. Along the Rhine in Germany, a castle was either made for show or as a fortress. Here in the south of France, they are going for a combination of the two. The location and surroundings would have made this "home" totally inaccessible from all but for one controlled narrow access road. Without the appearance of hostility, the structure appeared welcoming despite the elaborate and clearly visible defenses.

In the great room of the house, with a view of the moon-lit ocean along one entire wall, Carl Wilhelm Naundorff de Bourbon XII, a handsome and distinguished-looking gentleman, despite the round face and small pointed chin, was entertaining a small group of people, all seated near the open doors to the patio.

Laughing with the others, he excuses himself to answer his cell phone. Two of the younger women connect eyes with each other and then follow their host longingly, as he walks out of the room. Speaking in French, he sees the number and responds, "Bonjour ami." After a pause, "Something has been moved. I hope you can find it." He listens, "Yes, I am aware that is a possibility. Are you able to find him? Will this interfere with anything, like, for example, that other matter?"

"You know I didn't approve of what he was doing on the side don't you?" Again waiting, "I agree. Such a pity." Then turning serious while checking over his shoulder to see if the group is paying attention. Seeing that both of the younger women are watching him smiling, he smiles back coyly, turns his back on the small group of prying eyes and finishes the call, "I count on your discretion then, that It will not affect the schedule. Au revoir." He disconnects and walks back to the small group, both women still watching with willing smiles as he approaches. He apologizes courteously, "Business! I promise, no more interruptions."

As the party wears on someone comments about the Roman numeral on the end of his name. Carl jokes easily despite his discomfort at the untold story, he responded, "I wish I could get rid of it. When the radical black Muslim Malcolm X came to Europe in the 1970's they called him Malcolm the Tenth. It really doesn't mean much anymore other than to distinguish my father from me." While in his heart, the opposite was actually true. Carl held onto the firm belief that he was a direct descendent of the last French king, Louis XVI. His life revolved around returning his family to the pride and honor due them. Already a member of the French house of parliament, Mr. Naundorff de Bourbon has made many political allies with the well-placed honorarium, gift or invitation. Or, as here, a much-coveted invitation to his splendid house for the weekend. People from Washington, DC; Hollywood; Moscow and many other centers of power coveted the invitation.

For example, of the six people present, two were CEOs of international conglomerates. They brought with them their beautiful young trophy wives, whose sole interest was to trade up and become the fourth wife of their host and the closest thing to French royalty remaining after the execution of his alleged ancestor. The other two were from America: a somewhat famous Senator Robert W. Carter, who had a remote opportunity to become the next president of the United States, and his wife with the bedroom eyes. Fully ten years older that the other two women and yet infinitely more interesting--- Partly because she was absolutely exquisite and partly because she was apparently not interested in Carl.

Chapter 9

At midnight, when the senator asked his host's leave to go to bed, Carl apologized for keeping them and bid them all adieu. The senator took his beautiful wife's hand and led her into the hallway and across to their exquisite room. The other couples lagged momentarily as both of the women still attempted to maintain eye contact with their host. He smiled and led them into the hallway. Turning back to them part of the way down the hall toward his suite, he said, "Please, my house is your house. Explore anything that isn't locked." At that he winked coyly, and headed down the corridor toward his suite.

The need for sleep is universal. One of the family traits nurtured by Carl's ancestry for the past several hundred years had been to determine how to program one's own mind and body to skip the normal sleep protocol and leap headlong into deep, non-rapid eye-movement sleep. Having trained his mind and body like a zen master, Carl found that current break-though's in prescription drugs which reduced the time for a trained mind to achieve NRE sleep further reduced his overall need for sleep to just a couple of hours per night. Less, when necessary. Tonight it was not necessary, but the time difference between the southern coast of France and Los Angeles was nine hours, so being awake until four or five o'clock in the morning allowed him to be awake most of an extended business day in any city in the United States. Thus, at midnight, it was only three o'clock in the afternoon in Los Angeles when he sent an encrypted text and then dialed his phone. His call is answered immediately.

"Yes sir."

"What is happening?"

"I've sent for a team. They will be in place within the hour. We'll need to clean out the whole thing."

"I agree."

"I will call when we are set."

"Make sure to take care of our missing friend."

The meaning was crystal clear, "Yes sir."

Back in Los Angeles, Ernie Alvarez is sipping a Coke Zero and playing a video game when he checks his watch. Realizing he is late, he reaches for his phone and hits redial. After a moment the same voice answers curtly, "Demitre."

Despite thinking, "Who the hell is Demitre?" Ernie says, "Hey, he stopped."

Demitre asks, "Do you have the coordinates?"

"Yes sir. Am I supposed to be doing this?"

Demitre asks, "Do you want to make a great deal of money?" Before he can answer, Demitre continues, "I'll pay you ten thousand dollars to turn off the signal to that computer and push the special red button with your mouse that shows up on your screen. And then wait for my call. OK?"

"Sure."

He obeys after Demitre hangs up and when the red button appears, below it the screen says, "Destruct." He hesitates for a few minutes, conflicted about the reality and permanence of the word and then presses the button.

Chapter 10

Back in the Mobile home, standing in the living room, the three men whispering, Albert tells Robert, "You popped him. Damn, you broke his nose."

"It figures, A fucking lawyer AND a pervert. Boy it really felt good."

Evan laughs at Robert, "A twofer!"

Albert admonishes, "Hold it down, let's get Justin and set some ground rules. We don't even know what we want to do with him." They walk to the door, and as Robert turns the nob there is an explosion outside of the mobile home that shakes the entire structure violently. Stunned briefly, they all run outside. Justin's "little shop", their 10-by-10-foot shed, has been blown to bits. The debris is spread generally away from the mobile home across the 70-foot-wide open area. There is no fire, but the explosion has scorched the side of the mobile home. Robert is first to ask, "Justin? Where's Justin." The shed has been folded open from the inside, whatever is left of the four walls are laid flat and singed black on the inside. Electronics are spread everywhere, with the larger pieces out to about 25 feet.

All Albert can say is, "Shit. Justin. What did you do man?"

From behind them, there is a voice, "What the hell did you do to the shed?"

Startled, the three turn to see Justin zipping up his pants, with a newspaper tucked under his arm. Evan and Albert grab him and hug him, Albert saying, "Dude, we thought we'd lost you."

Justin reiterates, "I ask, what the hell did you do to the shed?"

Robert asks, "Us? None of us has even been in there since we got Lloyd."

Justin suddenly comes to a realization, "Holy shit. It was the computer. If I didn't have to pinch a loaf, I'd be dead!"

"The computer?" the three respond simultaneously.

Justin shrugs, "That's not the worst, I launched the entire drive into my iCloud except one little part that I couldn't open. Some proprietary files that looked like they were very specialized. If there was a bomb, I can guarantee two things; first that they know where we are right now and that someone is coming here shortly to see who interfered with their cash flow."

Albert looks at the other three, "What are we gonna do with Lloyd?"

Justin considers and says, "We leave him he dies, we take him, we don't have anyplace to put him. We turn him over to the police, we probably go to prison for kidnapping. We let him go, he's out of business. AND his boss is pissed, at least if he has a boss."

Robert is upset, "Let him go? Are you serious?"

Albert says, "He's made. He knows it. We got his gear. Well, his gear is not going to work anyway." pointing at the debris spread across the field.

Robert chuckles sarcastically.

Evan adds, "Justin got his account information. I say we move his cash to Bolivia or Estonia to a child services fund."

"Just let him go. Here's his car, right here, he can drive home," Justin logics.

Robert is devastated, "Let him go?"

Justin regrets, "We didn't plan what we were going to do. We're not killers, that is our option. Like Albert said, He's made. He's out of business."

Albert adds, "So we untie him and tell him we're sending him home."

Justin adds, "Yup, and we do it quickly so we can get out of here, too."

In the room Lloyd is frightened out of his mind. "Don't blow me up. Please! I'll tell you whatever you want to know."

Justin asks calmly, "Who gave you that computer?"

Lloyd freezes, adding two plus two, "The computer blew up on its own, right?" They look at each other and Lloyd knows he's right, so continues, "Then we need to get out of here and you need to crawl into a hole and pray that they don't find you."

Evan asks, "Who?"

Lloyd starts, "If you untie me, I'll tell you on my way out. If you don't untie me, then I'll take it with me to my soon-to-be grave."

Robert walks out of the room, pissed, as Albert, Taser in hand, cuts the binds and Lloyd starts talking. "The boogie man. If you don't believe in the devil, ... "Albert raises the Taser threateningly, "OK, I don't know his name and that's the truth. I don't know how you found me, but you'll never find him. He may be in politics, or he may just be a powerful guy. It's one or the other. They're too high-tech for the mob, the mob is all Neanderthals by comparison. Trust me, I know. I just know they stage accidents and nobody lives without their blessing. Remember John Travolta in "Swordfish"? He would be the "good guy" next to this guy."

Lloyd is now untied and walking out the front door of the mobile home massaging his wrists. He continues, "If you're smart, you'll wipe this place down and move to South America, which is what I am doing right now. My keys."

Evan tosses him his keys and Lloyd continues looking directly at Robert, "Fuck you very much for destroying my life."

Robert draws back to slug him and Lloyd flinches and

runs to his car, gets in and drives toward the PCH. Robert flips him off. "Pervert. Lawyer!"

Evan asks, "Well?"

Albert says, "We clean this place and -- wait a minute, … How long has it been, two hours total since we got shit head?"

Justin responds looking at his watch, "It seems like more than two hours, but it was less. Maybe an hour. As for evidence from this place, If they want DNA they're gonna get it. If they don't, well there's not much here. Let's make a sweep, turn on the security stuff and drop all this drama. Aren't we supposed to take the girls out to dinner tonight?"

They all move toward the door and walk inside. Albert adds, "Oh, yeah. Get the gloves, let's make this quick."

Chapter 11

Befitting Monsieur Naundorff's exquisite home, the master suite is filled with genuine French artifacts, including a museum-quality bedroom set., with one deception. One that is difficult to notice without actually being told that there were no king-sized beds made during the reign of Louis XIV. The workmanship is magnificent. The inlays and moldings on the bed itself exactly mimic the rest of the perfectly matched furniture, down to the engraver's signature, except for the first initial of the previous craftsman extraordinaire. The reason is that this particular piece was made by the descendants of the original craftsman, and other than the size, was made to the exact family-maintained specifications. In an adjacent alcove in the magnificent room, next to one of the two the fireplaces, Carl is seated at the beautifully carved Louis XIV desk in the matching chair.

Hearing a knock at the door, he is simultaneously annoyed at the intrusion and intrigued to see what secret offerings or pleasures he was to be offered.

At the door, the most perfect woman he has seen in years is holding an empty champagne glass as if presenting it to Carl. "Mister Naundorff," Senators Robert W. Carter's wife, Eileen, asks coyly, "What does a girl need to do around here to get a glass of champagne?"

Unsurprised but yet pleased that she was at his door, he acts surprised, steps aside and says, "Please, it's Carl. I generally don't trouble the staff at this hour, but I can offer you a rather excellent Claret that I have here fully decanted. I was just going to sample it myself. It's from my own small vineyard in Bordeaux."

She sweeps past him and saunters to the fireplace past his desk where the decanter is still breathing. "Two glasses, were you expecting someone?"

Carl smiles. Unwilling to say the truth that he had hoped she would come, he lied, "The proper decorum for European wait staff is to bring two glasses. This because of a stupid stigma about drinking alone."

She sets her glass on the mantle and sits on the settee next to the fire and wraps her arms around herself and lies, "The fireplace doesn't give off much heat."

He pours two glasses of the Claret, picks them up without answering her small talk and hands her a glass before sitting on the edge of the settee. "I am a very practical man. I have few needs." He sips the Claret and smiles as it rolls across his tongue. "So when I want something, I get to the point. I have you in a compromising set of circumstances, in a position where it would simply be your word against mine."She interrupts him with a smile and a wink. He collects himself and continues. "I shall be direct. What would it cost me to have you remove all of your clothing?"

She stands without hesitation and pushes the thin straps of her gown, allowing it to drop freely to the floor, wearing nothing underneath. Carl, believing that no one is perfect, acknowledges in his mind that she was in fact amazingly close. He says to her in absolute honesty, "Exquisite."

She walks to him and takes his hand, leads him to the magnificent bed and turns him so he can sit on the bed easily, which he does without further prompting. She then leans in and whispers into his ear, "I would do anything to help my husband become the next President of the United States."

He smiles broadly, "I would have done that anyway. I believe your husband is the "perfect" man for the job. You have my personal guarantee,.."

She interrupts him by placing her first finger gently on his lips, and then coyly saying, "Don't say that yet." She winks and continues, "I might need to come and remind you sometime."

Carl pulls her closer and kisses both of her nipples gently and draws her down beside him on the bed.

Later, in the afterglow, she apologizes, "I've been gone too long. I've gotta go back to my husband. He sleeps the sleep of the innocent, I'm afraid."

Carl smiles and says, "'I've gotta'. I've gotta,... I love Americans and their colloquialisms."

She gets up and walks to where her gown dropped and pulls it up over her shoulders. Carl gets up and walks naked to an armoire and pulls one door open. Selecting a wrap, he brings it to her and wraps it around her shoulders saying, "It can get chilly. It would look better if you had a wrap. Fewer questions." She smiles and they kiss at the door and she is gone. He walks calmly back to the armoire and puts on an elegant robe. Then he walks to his desk and boots up his Mac.

At the senator's room, she inches the door open and enters the suite, quietly slipping into the bathroom to freshen up. Even in the near dark, it is obvious that the room is appointed perfectly in every detail. After a few minutes, she comes out and slips off her gown to hang it up on a rack near the settee. She then grabs a simple nighty from the rack to put on, as a voice comes from the bed. "Don't! Please, I want to see you naked."

She turns, flushed, as he stares at her for a moment. Then he asks, "Did he go for it?"

She gives him a sly wink and walks toward him slowly and says, "Did you doubt me? Have I ever failed?"

The senator smiles as he pulls her to him and kisses her

flat stomach and says, "No, darling, you have never failed me." She smiles at the top of his head and slides over beside him in the bed.

In Carl's room, at that exact moment, he is staring at the replay of the scene with Eileen. He is watching carefully at the part where she stands and pushes the thin straps of her gown, allowing it to drop freely to the floor. Carl says, "Exquisite," at the exact instant that he says it on the video screen.

On the monitor, she walks to him and takes his hand and leads him to the bed and turns him and he sits on the edge of the bed. Carl cranks up the volume when she leans in and whispers into his ear, "I would do anything to help my husband become the next President of the United States."

Chapter 12

Four hours later, the four plus their beautiful wives are seated at Geoffrey's in Malibu sipping an apéritif and coffee after dinner and laughing about the panic and drama of the day. Seated so that they could converse privately despite the semi public location, Albert looks at Barbara and says, "So if he loaded his own computer with explosives, then he's a world-class actor. What a show. He was scared. And you should have seen Robert. We were like "bad cop, horrible cop'."

Robert interrupts, "I haven't punched anyone since high school. It felt wonderful."

Cherry raises her hand, "Whoa mister, don't be getting any ideas about hitting. At least as long as you sleep next to me and there are all those sharp knives in the kitchen."

The group laughs, and Robert kisses her lovingly and gets up, "I gotta see a man about a horse." He then walks through the bar to the restroom. On the Television, he sees Action News showing footage of a house burning on PCH and continues past to the men's restroom. On his way back, the words "Malibu Fire" stretch across the screen, and he pauses realizing that he has probably driven past the house now burning hundreds of, ... "Shit!"

He hurries back to the table and interrupts Evelyn, Justin's wife as she is talking about a movie that she and Justin had seen. "Hold on, I'm sorry." Robert looks deathly serious, "I think Lloyd burned his house down."

The other seven simultaneously gasp, "What?"

"It's on the news, and I'm pretty sure it's his house."

They lean in, and Albert states, "Two possibilities, or three, actually. The one I almost missed, he had an accident, or he did it or the devil did it."

Mary asks, "The devil?"

Justin responds, "That's what he made him sound like. Look, he's busted, he has a stash of cash in Europe, he probably is at risk from the guys that buy that crap. I say, if there's nobody in the house, he did it and ran. Ready to collect the insurance money from where ever he lands." They all agree and laugh about it, but not as fully or freely as before.

Barbara shakes her head and says, "Bizarre."

Chapter 13

Ernie, still in the room with the electronics, answers his cell phone. This time he is all business. "Yes sir. I did as you asked. I ran a full diagnostics on everything we had and traced every lead. Whoever hacked it was good, probably better than me. The only tiny slice of ID I got was from some home-made gear. I tracked to a hacker, in Lancaster. Yes sir, California. Lancaster, California. Named Peter Forrest. I've heard about him."

He presses the speaker phone, and the same voice as before says, "Is he capable of doing this?"

Ernie thinks before speaking, "He builds stuff. Quality stuff on a budget. But I would guess that, yes, he could do it."

"How far away is Lancaster?'

"Two hours. Give or take."

"Drive to Lancaster now. I will have someone contact you there in exactly two hours. Clear?"

"Sir I, ..."

"You will be paid very well when you arrive and you will earn my thanks."

Ernie smiles broadly as the phone clicks dead, even though the tiny alarm in his head that detects right and wrong is beeping loudly. He stands up and spins around, still a touch nervous, and he tries to bolster himself by saying loudly, "Who's the man? I'm the man!"

Exactly two hours later, as Ernie pulls into an AM/PM for an energy drink, his phone rings. Assuming these will be very serious people, he puts on his most helpful demeanor, breaths deeply and answers, "Ernie here," immediately thinking, "Should I have said Ernest?'

A new voice answers and says, "We are two blocks from you, do you have the address?"

Wondering only briefly how they could tell how close they were to him, he responds, "We're about a minute away from his house from where I am."

"Lock your car and wait, we are in a black GMC Suburban coming around the corner now." The line goes dead as Ernie sees the totally politically incorrect vehicle turn into the parking area -- the same cliché vehicle they use to excess in movies to represent the dark forces. He shudders at the thought as he walks over. They open the door, and he raises his hand to wave and immediately feels stupid about it. Ernie gets in and they drive away immediately. Ernie hands the passenger in the front seat the paper with the address and says to the driver, "Turn at the next corner, right, then it's just at the end of the street."

They follow his instructions and turn down a dark and

sparsely populated street outside the mainstream of the burgeoning town. One of the four people in the SUV hands a headset to Ernie, and he slaps it to his head immediately hearing information about the property. Having a moment to look around to see the four men he is riding with, Ernie ascertains that they at least appear to be serious men. They are wearing matching black windbreakers covering body armor and sophisticated belts with gismos and gadgets -- which excites Ernie more than he would believe possible. "Cool, what do you want me to do?" He knows that he may be inside at the moment, but he is still an outsider to these hardened men.

The leader is clearly, Pavel, a grizzled man with scars and a crewcut appears to be in his 50's. Pulling an unlit cigarette from his mouth, he says, in his Russian accent, "Nothing until we tell you to come in." Then to the others as the SUV rolls to a stop in Russian, "Let's do it."

Without saying anything, or at least not on the channel that Ernie is set on, they all pull their night vision goggles over their heads and moving in separate trajectories. Two of the men moving to surround the small house and two entering the house in full stealth mode. There is complete silence over the headset until a key is clicked three times and he hears the leader say over his earpiece, "He's down. Ernie, come in now, it is safe."

Ernie gets out flattered that they are concerned about

his safety but uncertain about the prospect of seeing a dead body. As such, he walks with some trepidation to the front door, stopping long enough to feel stupid when he tries to knock as the door is opened and he is handed a pair of rubber gloves. The man handing him the gloves says, "Put these on." Obeying without question -- after all this is unquestionably a crime scene -- he enters and follows the man in front of him to the back.

Instantly, he recognizes the room as being similar to his own hacker's fortress of solitude where he had happily squandered his time. The gear is semi-professional, nowhere near as good as what he has back at the shop, but better than he had at home by a long shot. The hacker is quivering slightly on the floor, and one of the attackers is folding a Taser into a pocket on his vest, so Ernie assumes he is alive but out of commission. A sigh of relief washes over him and he steps over the hacker to see what he can find.

"He knew you guys were on the way in." Ernie perceived without looking that he had just earned their respect. Pointing to a light on one of the screens he says, "See that light, that's probably from the backyard or a window you set off." He worked and talked, "Motion detector if it was me. He set out a surge of some kind, like a hacker distress call. A spike that would signal whoever he might want to be protecting that there is a problem. Probably Homeland

Security or someplace that would report it in the newspaper." Still inspecting, he realizes, "This can't be our guy. But he knew him. He may be the builder of a piece of equipment that our guy hooked up, that's all. This guy, nope, he's been here all day. Never left according to this readout."

Pavel says curtly, "Take his equipment. Unhook everything and we'll leave."

As soon as the gear is removed, one of the men pulls a syringe from a zipper case and watches as Ernie leaves the room. Ernie carries a small piece of gear to the SUV and gets in.

As they drop him at his car, the man next to him hands him an envelope, which he peeks into as they drive away. Inside the envelope he sees an inch and a half of hundred dollar bills. "Whoa."

Chapter 14

Justin and Evelyn, a truly loving couple, despite being two completely diverse people, drive home quietly discussing the fire. Evelyn suggests, "Maybe there is something on the news."

Justin reaches over and turns on KNX news radio and has trouble finding a signal. Then, suddenly, he gets the signal and the voice on the radio says, "Well, we're back on the air again. Off the air for the first time in almost 20 years, and it's the first time that we are the news. We are being told that our communication center has been spiked, or, more precisely, targeted with a signal burst so strong that it temporarily knocked KNX news radio off the air. Our apologies to anyone who was inconvenienced by this, but it was pretty darn inconvenient to us too."

As they pull into the driveway and open the garage door, Justin says, "Sorry love. That spike was probably a signal and I need to check it out."

They walk into the house, kiss and part company. Evelyn says, "I'm going to call Barbara and let them know."

"Hey, tell them it might be nothing, but it's just suspicious, OK. Thanks."

By four o'clock in the morning, all four of the men are in

Justin's basement and the four women are sound asleep because they have real jobs. Albert is reading a stack of printouts as Robert and Evan are napping in overstuffed chairs against the wall. Justin flexes his back and stands to stretch and says, "He's dead. The report says Peter Forrest had a heart attack, but I doubt it."

Albert asks, "Why? From what you said, he was a forty-year-old, over weight guy who never left his house. He sends out a hacker's distress signal and keels over."

"If he had a heart attack he would call 911, just like you or me. The hacker's distress is for everyone else. He spiked a radio station knowing it would make the news to warn us he was under attack. He was killed."

Albert asks, "What does that have to do with us?"

Justin sighs and responds, "Part of the equipment that I hooked up to that computer that blew up at the trailer, was Peter's. I bought it from him."

Albert, confused asks, "And 'they' did this?" Albert wakes Evan and Robert and says, "Justin is convinced his guy was murdered and the Devil is real."

Justin interrupts, "That's not what I said."

Robert looks at them both, and Evan rubs his face as Albert responds, "Then what? A bunch of coincidence? The only guy that could be connected to the problem sets off a warning spike and has a non-accidental heart attack. Then the house we were in today, I mean yesterday, had a gas leak and burned to the ground, no body found and the owner has disappeared." The room is silent.

Evan asks the obvious to Justin, "What are the chances that they'll find you?"

Justin, still standing, sits back down and says, "I don't even use the closest cell tower."

Robert asks, "I'm just wondering if anyone went up to the mobile home."

Justin turns, surprised, and points at Robert, "Me too!" Then reaches over to a bank of buttons and presses several as one of his smaller monitors lights up with views of the mobile home, interior and exterior.

On another panel he presses a button and says, "This should jump to anything in the yard and then sync the cameras." The static on the screen is somehow soothing to the four tired men until darkness appears and then self-adjusts to the ambient lighting. In the image, a black GMC Suburban appears and the time frame indicates 7:41 PM. The interior camera clicks on, and they watch four armed men approach the mobile home, two of whom enter as the other two walk around the perimeter.

Robert is the first to speak, "Night vision goggles, just after dark." No one else speaks.

The interior camera shows the two men searching the trailer carefully and then coming back out to the living area. One points to the kitchen as the other two men join them from outside. The same one points to the rear rooms, and the other three move away quickly into the rooms. He then moves into the kitchen area.

Robert asks, "What are they doing?" Still no response. The man in the kitchen reaches behind the gas oven and jerks something away from the wall.

Evan says, "Gas?"

Robert, guessing, says, "Yup."

The four men then walk to the front door and open it. Three walk out as the fourth hooks something up to the door. Albert asks, "Blasting cap?"

Justin answers, "Could be a match and a striker. A lighter or something either simple or sophisticated. Anything to cause a spark when someone opens the door."

Robert makes an explosion with his fists and says, "Boom."

The exterior camera shows the four men get in the SUV and drive away.

Evan realizes suddenly, "Someone is trying to make our deaths look like an accident."

Albert checks his watch and realizes, "So by now the gas has been on for six-plus hours. I would say that place is screwed. Where we gonna play cards"

Justin smiles and says with the worst possible accent, "Au Contraire mon frere."

Evan smiles, "I love it when you speak French."

Justin points to a computer screen that displays a residential electric setup and sets his finger on a button that says "Remote Rapid Ventilation." "That would be the gizmo. The question is do we want to save the trailer or let them think they got us? I say we sleep on it. They can't expect us to go backup there for a while."

Chapter 15

Unable to sleep in airplanes, the situation was made worse when he found out that first class had been filled by half of an American soccer team headed for a match in Zagreb. As such, the normal suffering which Lloyd tolerates on his trips was magnified in the tiny coach seat jammed together with too many stinking bodies and screaming children.

Lloyd is exhausted as he gratefully pulls away from the Zagreb Airport. Ignoring the wonders of Eastern European culture, Lloyd waives off the repeated offers from the cab driver and the cab takes him directly to the Regent Esplanade Zagreb. After repeatedly trying to leave a cash deposit, the hotel insists on a credit card, and Lloyd, painfully fatigued, eventually relents and hands over his American Express card. Finally in his room, without unpacking or taking off his two-day-old clothing, Lloyd crawls on top of his bed and is sound asleep the instant his head touches the pillow.

Half a world away, Ernie scans a screen that was triggered on one of his monitors, "Well, well, there you are, you Wascally Wabbit. Just like he said you would be." He sends an encrypted email with the particulars and then dials his phone and waits for the reply. "One ringy dingy, two ringy dingy."

"Demitre."

"Yes sir, your friend showed up in Croatia. I sent you the particulars just like you wanted."

"Thank you, Ernest. You do excellent work. I will tell my superiors of your diligence and efforts." Demitre disconnects and opens an encryption program and then opens the email. He forwards the email encrypted and dials his phone.

Carl is seated at his desk when his cell phone rings. His door knocks at the same time so he walks to the door as he answers, "Yes?" Opening the door, he sees Eileen Carter standing outside the door with a bottle of champagne. Carl puts his finger to his lips for her to be quiet and winks, getting out of the way and waiving her into the room.

On the other end of the phone, Demitre says, "I found your long-lost friend and sent you the information in an email."

Carl pulls Eileen to him and kisses her briefly on the lips before saying. "Excellent. Where?" Eileen steps back, and again moves the small straps allowing the gown to drop to the floor. Carl cannot help himself and says, "Exquisite."

Demitre asks, "Sir?"

Carl ignores him and asks, "Where would he be then?"

Demitre, sensing that Carl is otherwise occupied and the need for discretion, says, "In Zagreb sir."

Carl asks, "Isn't that sort of your area of expertise?"

Demitre smiles and says, "Yes sir, I can get workers to the area within the next couple of hours. I have a many good people in the area. It will be handled."

Carl looks at Eileen and says to her and top the phone, "You have become most useful. Thank you very much for your kind assistance."

Eileen steps forward and wraps her arms around Carl pressing her firm body tightly into his silk robe.

Demitre sends the same encrypted email again and calls a different number. Then in Russian he says, "I have sent an email with a name and particulars. He is a very special friend, and he should be extended every courtesy. What would be the time frame to Zagreb?"

A small and heavily scarred man seated at a computer terminal opens the email and says, "Another fat American? Yes, I will do something special. We have a local ceremony that I am sure he would enjoy. We can pick him up within an hour."

At the Regent Esplanade Zagreb, the same heavily scarred man, standing with three large friends, hands a bellhop with his luggage cart a stack of Euros and the bellhop uses his key to open the door to Lloyd's hotel room. He and his friends enter the room with the luggage cart and watch until the bellhop is completely gone from view.

Among the many other amenities Croatia offers to the traveler, in the mountains of Croatia are fields filled with land mines, a remnants from years of civil wars. Invisible to the naked eye, they wait patiently to announce their violent intent. Grown over with grass and flowers, the fields have become beautiful, as innocent and pure in appearance as any meadows Lloyd may have visited in his youth.

As Lloyd awakens from his drug-addled sleep, he is shocked to find himself in the middle one of these meadows.. A note is tied to his chest with a map on the back. The map has an X which apparently marks his location, and the note reads simply, "Good Luck."

Chapter 16

Samuel Haywood was content, fishing in a place where fish might not interfere with his down time. Today, he was infinitely more interested in getting to know his six-year-old grandson, Mike.

Forgiven by his family for his stupidity, which had almost cost him his retirement, marriage and sanity, he was now reconciled with his abandoned wife and two daughters, retired from the FBI and back home. Boy did that sound good right now! "Home!" If he was lucky, he would earn enough running his little one-man PI office, and pray that his ex-wife would eventually be more than an ex. A situation that was all his fault, hearing the call of the big city and the big time in the FBI, when he knew that she would never move. Despite his obstinance, he had acquired a few friends, a commodity which he unfortunately had learned to live without for a time. They had taught him to listen to his own heart and probably saved him from himself.

His daydream shattered suddenly, as Mike's bobber bobs and Sam sets down his rod to stand behind his grandson for moral support. "Not too quick, let him set the hook." Suddenly the bobber dips and runs as far as the inexpensive bamboo rod will allow. "Now you've got him!"

The battle with the tiny fish lasts only seconds, but Sam knows they will be able to talk about this day for the rest of their lives. Mike turns to his grandfather and asks, "Do we have to take him home?"

Sam smiles broadly and responds, "Let's let him go and come back and catch him again when he's bigger, OK?"

Mike smiles broadly and nods, and they start to put everything away. Concerned, Mike asks, "Will you tell momma how little he was?"

Sam laughs and says, "You really don't know anything about fishing do you. Fish are always bigger in the stories. Here, hold him up in front of you and I'll take a picture." Sam instructs him to stand still and hold the fish out at an angle in front of him. Mike obliges, and Sam's trustee Blackberry snaps a picture that makes the fish look much bigger, just as it rings.

One minute earlier and he would have simply not answered, but the moment was gone and he checked the number. Seeing that it was his friends in Malibu, he smiled and answered, "Haywood Investigations, You stab em we slab em."

The four are on Justin's speaker phone, and Robert asks, "Is that your snappy new slogan, there, Special Agent Haywood?"

"It was that or 'Make your Bullshit Problems My Bullshit Problems. What do you think?'"

Albert asks seriously, "Did you know what you were sending us?"

Haywood withdraws a bit and asks, "Can I call you back in 20 minutes, I need to drop off my grandson at home."

"OK, but plan on coming down and going to work."

Twenty-five minutes later, picture having been sent to Mike's momma and daddy by text, Sam knocks on the door with some trepidation and does not step in as his grandson scoots past Margaret when she opens the door. "I'm probably going to have to go on a job in Malibu. I'm sorry, until my pension comes through I ..."

Margaret takes his hand warmly and says, "No apologies needed. Go to work and come back when you can." Relieved by her gracious response, Sam raises her hand and kisses it before going back to his car.

Sam calls back as he gets back in his car, which is parked out in front of Margaret's house. After brief amenities, he asks Justin "So what's the matter Wonder Boy? Can't find out who made the picture?"

Justin takes a breath and starts, "We want to hire you to help us with this. We're in over our heads and ..."

Albert interrupts, "It's worse than that. We may be in trouble."

"With the law?"

Robert offers, "With the devil."

Albert asks, "Can you tell your wife that you got a case

that will pay enough to launch your business and just come down here so we can explain it to you face to face?"

Haywood opens the car door and walks toward his ex-wife's door. "I'm on my way. What time are the flights?"

Justin responds, "You're booked on the 12:45 PM flight. Are you going to be able to make it?"

Quick calculations, "Yeah I live near SeaTac, so I should have time for lunch even."

Justin interrupts, "Save it, you're in first class, and the salmon of Alaska Air is pretty good. Start the clock and don't give us any crap. You work for us now."

Obediently, Haywood responds, "Yes sir!"

Chapter 17

Justin was right about the salmon on the airplane and the two of them exchanged photos while in the air. Haywood sent the photo of his grandson with the fish, and Justin sent a video of the four armed men at the mobile home. The seriousness of the situation was crystal clear, even if the video was a touch grainy despite being on the tiny Blackberry screen. The cryptic text was also crystal clear: "Our fish was a small fish and the big fish is defending territory aggressively. We think we are safe in the boat, but it depends on how big the fish turns out to be." They're sure they are safe for now, but they don't know what they're up against.

What in the world happened? Haywood had simply tried to give them a reason to get out of bed. Now their lives may be at risk.

At the airport, the four picked up Haywood and they moved toward the baggage claim area updating each other on their lives.

In Evan's Audi V8, the five friends finished hellos and then the four laid out what little they knew. Haywood withheld questions until they were finished.

"How did they get to the guy in Lancaster?"

Justin sighs, "When I moved some gear to the shed... "

Evan interrupts, "May it rest in pieces."

Justin rolls his eyes and continues, "I knew him from when he was a monster hacker. I was throwing him a bone when I bought some gear off of him. He charged me too much, I paid it -- I was rolling in it by then. It was a universal interface and it was sweet. Just something I didn't want to take the time to build myself." Robert is rolling his hands in an effort to get Justin on point. "Yeah Yeah, He was proud of it so he put his hacker ID on it just in case someone gave a shit."

Haywood did, so he asks, "You ever do that?"

"Yeah, when I was twelve. It takes so long to get a copyright, by the time you get it through the application process, the next big thing is out there, so we all did it."

Haywood, partly joking, "Twelve? Were you just kidding about the twelve part?"

Justin responds joking, "No, I think that was when I invented the weenie pump for Robert."

Robert retorts, "You never get to the point! People are dying here. Get to the point."

Haywood moves on, "So the mobile home is still gassed?"

Albert responds, "Justin made a good point. Is it better that they think we're dead? That was the question on the table when we decided to call you."

Haywood ponders, "I see a couple of risks. To start, whoever goes out there to fix it will be found out. If you hire someone, it can be traced. There are people that know about us. The risk is too high to send a stranger. So let's look at the video again."

At Justin's house, Haywood and Evelyn say high as the rest of the pack scurry to the basement. When he arrives, the video is booted and Haywood is offered the seat directly in front of one of the monitors.

Justin presses a button on the panel.

The static on the screen is again somehow soothing, until darkness appears and then self-adjusts to the ambient lighting. In the image, a black GMC suburban appears and the time frame indicates 7:41. The interior camera clicks on, and they watch four armed men approach the mobile home and two enter as the other two walk around the outside of the mobile home.

Evan points out, "Night vision goggles, just after dark." Robert rolls his eyes.

The interior camera shows the two men searching the trailer carefully and then coming back out to the living area. One points to the kitchen as the other two men join them from outside the mobile home. The same one points to the rear rooms and the other three move away quickly into the rooms. The fourth man moves into the kitchen area. He reaches behind the gas oven and jerks something away from the wall.

The four men walk to the front door and open it. Three of the four walk out as the fourth hooks something up to the door. Albert asks, "We figured that was some kind of sparking thing? You know, something to cause a spark."

Back in the video, again,the four men get in the SUV and drive away. The time signature says 7:58 PM.

Haywood starts, "Wow, in and out in seventeen minutes. Pros, but who and from where? We never get a clear shot of the license plate, it's too dark to get a face or distinguishing marks. I'm going to guess they showed up that day from someplace else and did the deed. What time was the spike?"

Justin is stumped, "Uh, what time did we have dinner that night?"

Albert responds, "7:30? Great food horrible service, coffee and aperitifs, so out about 10, 10:30."

Haywood asks, "Could they get out to Lancaster in two hours?"

They confer and Evan nods, saying, "Easy."

Haywood presses his supposition, "So if the computer was moved about, what, 11:30 or 12, and they showed up by 7 PM, and if they hopped a commercial flight from somewhere."

Albert points out, "That's a lot of ifs."

Haywood nods and continues, "And the spike was after 10 pm, that means that if it's the same four guys, they got here some time in the afternoon and rolled out on the red eye, the same day." He looks at Justin, "Can you look at flight records and check my hypothesis?"

Justin smiles and turns around to a computer and starts the data entry. Haywood asks, "Is this the button to do the video again?"

Evan says, "Here I'll do it. What do you want to see?"

"First, I want to make sure that only four guys were there. Then see if any of them dropped or placed anything outside. Then assume that the plan was well thought out. So someone checked to see if there was a gas hookup at the property. That may be traceable. Then we decide if we can get more information out of the device before or after it explodes."

Robert asks, "So you think it needs to explode?"

"I'm leaning that way. But we have a limited window. When the shed blew up, it would scare anyone, so I figure we have a couple days before it will seem odd that it hasn't gone up. Oh, and let's assume also they might have the camera feed from your cameras at the mobile home, so we can't just walk up to the door either."

"So what do we do?"

Haywood looks at Justin working and says, "We need someone with a gift at math to compute how much gas would cause a showy explosion without actually killing anyone."

The other three nod, and Justin turns around and smiles. Haywood continues, "Justin needs to be here to shut off the video feed just in case the bomb is a dud."

Evan asks, "Well what about if the bomb is too big?"

Chapter 18

Ernie, again in the monitor station with a folded slice of pizza, is seated at one of the monitors. He dials a number on his cell phone, puts the phone on speaker and sets it down on the counter next to the keyboard. The phone is answered on the other end with a simple, "Yes?"

"Four people going to the trailer. You said to call."

"Yes, tell me what they do."

Ernie watches and says, "They're splitting up. Two at the door, and two going each direction around the trailer looking for something. OK, the two at the door are opening the door, wow. It blew up. Holly shit. They're goners. The video feed is out, no wait," it clicked back on, just the outside. "Two men down and one guy staggering up from the side and collapses. Woo, face first, he's gone. Where's the other guy? Oh! Video is back off. Jesus, what happened?"

"Not your concern. Thank you, you have been most useful. I will send you an additional bonus. Excellent work my friend, excellent."

Ernie makes sure the phone is hung up and stands casually, then breaks into a touchdown, celebration dance. "Who's the man? I'm the man! Who's the man? I'm the man!"

At the mobile home, they are still dusting themselves off and stripping off their layers of clothing. Everything is placed into garbage bags, and rubber gloves and earplugs are tossed into the same garbage bags. Haywood walks up from the front door area of the trailer with the remains of the sparking tool. He tells them what he has learned, "Low tech but clean. In a bigger explosion it would have burned up."

Albert shakes his head and pops out his earplugs, "I'm gonna talk to Justin about the gas ratio thing, though. My ears are ringing still."

Haywood's phone rings and he sees it's Justin's number, "Yeah, but speak up because I can't friggin hear." He presses the speaker button.

Justin starts right in, "We need to meet, and you guys need to get out of there." Slipping into a hillbilly accent, "Oh, by the way you guys got blowed up real good! Let's get a beer, OK?" and he clicks off the line.

Robert says, "Asshole!"

Evan adds, "That wasn't too cryptic was it?"

Haywood responds, "He wants us out of here, so where do you guys drink beers?"

At the sports bar, seated in the their same far corner, with designer ales dripping condensation, having been served from the near-freezing refrigerator, the four watch as Justin walks in and says, "Before you kill me, you have to see the video." He sits and holds up one finger for the bar tender, who nods his response, and Justin presses play and holds the phone so they can all see.

In the video, the four are going to the trailer. Two remain at the door and two go each direction around the trailer looking for something. Albert at the door reaches for the knob and starts opening the door. Suddenly the video feed ends and there is static on the screen. Robert reacts, "Holly shit. We blew up!" The video feed is out, then the video clicks back on, just the outside. Albert and Haywood are on their backs and not moving at all. Robert staggers in and falls over convincingly and Robert stands and says when he sees it, "Thank you very much, ladies and gentlemen of the academy."

All four of the others say in unison, "Boooo!" and throw peanuts at Robert as the video feed shuts off completely.

Justin asks, "Where's the fourth guy."

Evan responds, "I was dead behind the trailer."

Justin replies, Does that make sense to you?"

Haywood is impressed, "Honestly? I think he believes we're dead and will probably try to clean up any loose ends. I'm not sure how that helps us find whoever is behind this though. So why did you think we need to get out of there in such a hurry?"

Evan adds, "Yeah, I was still getting the crap and dust out of my hair." They all look at Justin.

"I did a run on credit cards, nothing out of the ordinary. I did a run on four guys coming from out of town and didn't find any that correlate to the time frame that we set."

Evan and Robert both are rolling their hands in the "get to the point" hand signal and Haywood laughs, "This is a tough room. Details are important!"

Justin says, "Thank you."

Robert adds, "If the details are important and not complete bullshit."

Albert looks at Justin, "Dude, what did you find?" Then thinking, "Crap, "Dude." Justin, I'm starting to sound like you!"

Justin smiles and continues, "When I ran three people, I got a bingo. Three different people from three different areas, all within two hours flight time. Meaning the fourth is local or at least drivable." He looks at Haywood, and Haywood nods for him to continue. "They all showed up within half an hour of each other, and the three were on a plane out of here just after midnight."

Evan considering the logistics, "What would something like that cost?"

Haywood shrugs, "A million, I don't know?"

Justin continues, "It says here that Lloyd's credit card shows up." He looks at Haywood, "Why the hell would he go to Croatia?"

Haywood responds, "High standard of living, lots of beautiful women with low moral standards and no extradition agreement with the U.S. Low crime rate, friendly to Americans. Lots of reasons really -- the biggie is they have no extradition agreement with the U.S."

Albert perplexed, "How the heck do you find out all of this stuff?"

Haywood shrugs, "Wikipedia."

Haywood responds, "With what my gut tells me, I'll bet the farm that our kiddie porn buddy dies violently in Croatia within a month."

Robert asks Haywood, "So you think that someone is after *us*?"

Haywood ponders out loud, "If it was me and I was cleaning house and I had already gone through everything I had already done, I would leave people that pulled the trigger, because the FBI is hard-pressed to offer them a deal. But I would get rid of any other loose ends that might be in the area."

Justin is already with his phone out typing on the tiny keys as fast as possible. "Hackers, snitches and watchers. Snitches and watchers I can't find. But I own hackers, and somebody did some exceptional work to find Forrest. He was a difficult target. It was probably someone that knew who he was."

Chapter 19

Ernie sits with one leg up on the desk and picks up another piece of pizza. He folds it long ways and puts the pointy end in his mouth east-coast style. One of the monitors beeps, and he scoots his rolling chair to that monitor and freezes, mid chew. "Oh shit." He starts to scramble and reaches over to a master switch and flips it. He then starts unplugging wires from a panel on the wall as fast as he can, "Oh, shit!" In the monitor, just before he unhooks the feed, is a black GMC Suburban, with the last of four getting out and gathering at the front door of an industrial complex. The last thing he does is lift the far rear panel of cheap soundproof ceiling tile, pick his laptop up, and crawl up on a filing cabinet and into the ceiling and put the ceiling tile back into place.

It is dusk, outside of a seventies-era industrial complex, and the four men, without night vision goggles, reach under their black windbreakers and check their weapons. The extremely ordinary concrete two-story complex surrounds an open area that sits like a postcard, with several mature jacaranda trees in full bloom. They walk to the green door marked "Plaza Security". The man in the lead inserts an electric lock-pick device into the dead bolt lock and almost instantly says, in an Eastern European accent, "Ready." He opens the door, and the four file in.

Inside the structure, they split up. The first man moves to disable the alarm system, while the second goes into the bathroom and checks for alarms or booby traps. The last two head down to the end of the long room checking under tables and around monitor stations that, up until a few seconds before, Ernie had been scooting around. As each finishes his assigned task, they regroup in the middle of the room and the leader, returning from the bathroom, picks up a piece of pizza, takes a bite and says in Russian, "Turn it over!" He pulls out his cell phone and hits redial as the other three upend everything in the room, searching every nook.

In the parking lot behind the structure, Ernie is sweating profusely as he runs to his car. He presses the button to open the door of his dependable dark brown 2002 Toyota Camry. He realizes that they have seen his car in Lancaster and can identify it. "Shit!" He puts his laptop on the passenger seat and checks his rear pocket for the envelope full of money, setting it on the seat and sliding it partway under the computer. He puts the key in the ignition of the vehicle and starts it up. He backs out of the parking area and pulls out onto the street, looking carefully both directions. At the first street, he turns left and then turns right and gets directly onto the southbound 101 freeway.

In the security office, the four men have torn the unit to shreds. One man using the handle of a broom, finally gets to the end, and when the last tile drops he yells in Russian, "Here."

The other three run to the spot and assist the first man in straightening a turned-over filling cabinet, and then Pavel, climbs on top of it. He levers himself to the ceiling and sees the access panel and opens it, yelling, still in Russian, "Out back."

The four run outside and around the building into the employee parking area and stop. Pavel pulls a cell phone-sized device off of a clip on his jacket and turns it on. After only a few seconds, he yells in Russian, "South!" and the four men run back to their car.

Ernie pulls off on the next exit at a Shell gas station next to a long-haul trailer that is getting ready to leave. He takes the envelope and opens it. He carefully pulls each bill out and shakes the envelope ejecting a small, computer chip-sized piece of electronics. Knowing instantly what he is looking at, he says, "Oh shit!" Thinking quickly, Ernie takes a piece of gum out of his pocket and starts chewing. Hearing the big rig being shifted into gear, he steps out of the car to a place where the driver cannot see him and presses the gum onto the computer chip and out of view from prying eyes, leans over and presses the gum and chip onto the bottom of the big rig. Sweating profusely, Ernie gets back in his car and takes a deep breath. Starting his car, Ernie makes a life-or-death decision by following the big rig to the freeway. The big rig turns right into the southbound onramp. Ernie then turns left for the onramp onto the freeway headed north and drives as fast as he feels is safe.

Chapter 20

Normally the visits at Evan's house are two groups separated boys and girls talking about whatever they will talk about. Today, the five friends and the four wives sit in a large circle as Haywood goes through the possibilities for their way forward. "Let's say we take what we have to the FBI. We have no idea what happened."

Albert protests, "That's not true, we stopped a child pornography ring."

Haywood continues, "What do you have besides a destroyed mobile home that in actuality, we blew up and a chance to show that you're connected to two murders?"

Barbara ask, "Two people? I don't understand?"

Justin speaks up, "Forrest, in Lancaster. Lloyd, in Croatia. That we know of."

Robert, "Already?"

Haywood adds reading a printout, "Yup. He stepped on a land mine."

Robert pops in, "So Croatia offers a high standard of living, lots of beautiful women with low moral standards, no extradition agreement, low crime rate, friendly to Americans and land mines. What else could you want."

Haywood continues with a reminder, "Plus a house

blown to bits here in Malibu. So how do we go to the authorities?"

Evan corrects him, "Lloyds house burned down."

Haywood adds, "Whatever."

Albert thinks about it, "So do you think we're in trouble?

Haywood continues with a reminder, "I'm pissed. And trust me, that's not a good thing." His stern look freezes the rest of them. "When I'm pissed, I have to call a friend and work out a plan. If you want me to go off the clock, I understand. But this is my fight now, same as yours. In fact, I kind of got you into this."

They don't hesitate. Barbara speaks as she often does, the decisive surgeon's mind at work, "We have money, we lack credibility. You have credibility as a retired FBI agent, for whatever that's worth. If you're on our payroll, then it looks like we're trying to do something credible." The others nod agreement. "That means we look more credible with you in the lead."

Haywood responds, "Ok, in the lead to where?

Justin remembers something, "When I did the phone call search of phone calls that might set up getting the hit men here, one common number seemed to be involved. Also, there is an encrypted file that was sent from that number to a number in the south of France and then to Zagreb, Croatia. I'm still working on the file, but I'm guessing it's information on Lloyd."

Haywood, interested, asks, "What area did he call from?"

Justin raises a single finger and says, "Interesting thing. He called at least once from the wi-fi at the Fairmont Miramar Hotel & Bungalows, in Santa Monica."

Robert and Evan agree, "Nice hotel."

Chapter 21

Demitre Velicoff sits casually on his balcony on Ocean Avenue at the luxurious Fairmont Miramar Hotel & Bungalows. His new employer believed that good people should be paid well. Especially those that were willing to do anything at all. Demitre was a problem solver. If Demitre was told to make a problem go away, people around the problem would wake up and wonder why there was a hole where a problem used to be. He knew that if he were ever discovered or arrested, the world would look to his previous employment with the Russian Mob and his new employer would be shielded and beyond reproach.

From Demitre's position, he was doing a less risky job for a great deal more money and he was in charge locally. The biggest factor was that he didn't have to deal with the constant threat of dissenting groups within his own organization, which tended to make things too fluid and fraught with danger. Here, he was soaking in the afternoon sun and sipping a designer pale ale, ecstatic that he had finally found that there were drinkable beers in America. But why did they all have to have such stupid names? It seemed that the more stupid the name, the better the beer. He wondered blankly if that was the rule.

Expecting the call, he stands after the first ring, steps into the room from the balcony and slides the door closed to cut off the traffic noise from Ocean Avenue. He says, "Yes sir, I have information." Having learned early on that his new boss loved the sound of his own voice, Demitre started quickly, which suited him fine as he was not a huge fan of talking on the phone. "There is a new player, a retired FBI agent that I have been observing this past year, Samuel Haywood. He is not to be discounted."

Concerned, Carl asks, "Retired? What is he doing if he is retired?"

"He runs a small investigation firm in Seattle."

"Seattle? That's over a thousand miles from Los Angeles. Who hired him?"

"That is not a public record, and I,... "

"ALRIGHT! Then to Mr. Alvarez, anything?"

"Not yet."

Carl takes a breath, "I have sent a new man. Very peculiar but talented. You may know him from Moscow. I heard he worked there for a while." Changing the subject, "Who ever it is, this Haywood, who is he working for and is there anything that can be linked to us?"

"No. Whatever they learned, they learned from Mr. Weber." Unsure as to his next step, "What do you want me to do, sir."

"Settle the new man and don't be seen. Do you have a

facility?"

"Yes, a lovely house in Venice. I am on my way there when we are done."

"Excellent, Make him feel appreciated. Mr. Alvarez was not your fault. He was a mistake, hired before you started for me and he will be dealt with shortly. Correct?" Without waiting for an answer, the connection is terminated.

Demitre dials his phone and waits for the answer and asks, "Pavel, did you find Mr. Alvarez yet?" Clearly upset by the response, he calms himself, "Then do what you can. He is a liability that we cannot afford to have reappear."

Demitre gathers his helmet and checks the room. He takes one more look out at the ocean and sets some clothing for the laundry service. He slips his motorcycle jacket over his always-present, old-fashioned police-issue shoulder holster and makes sure the door lock catches on his way out the door.

In the lobby, Demitre walks past a short man reading a newspaper wearing a faded red Washington Redskins cap, He doesn't notice the cell phone held mindlessly on a small hook on his finger, which is actually shooting video of Demitre's stroll across the lobby.

At the door, Demitre glances back with a chill shooting up his spine as if someone just walked across his grave. Seeing nothing suspicious, an old couple arguing with the concierge and a man with his face in the newspaper wearing his cell phone like a pinkie ring--he shakes off the feeling and walks out the door to where the valet has left his expensive motorcycle.

Playing back the brief video, Haywood asks himself, "Who are you and why would I recognize your face?"

Chapter 22

An odd-looking man walked from the secured part of the Los Angeles Thomas Bradley International terminal to the free air of Los Angeles. He was waif thin, six foot 4 inches tall, with a pasty complexion. His thick glasses set on the edge of his nose, his eyes continually darting about over the top of the frame. The suit he wore was clearly off the rack although he could afford Seville Row should he be so inclined. The overall appearance, which arguably he designed intentionally, was that he had lost significant weight recently from a devastating bout with an ailment du jour. A normal response to his appearance was, "Are you alright?" which also rang with the connotation in the "Bird Flu" era that one should take a wide birth around Edgar "The Weasel" Wessell. His appearance when combined with his last name and the inherent cruelty of schoolyard boys even in his native France, had long since been turned to an advantage, at least in Edgar's mind. Shunned until his growth spurt at age 14, when several boys had painfully determined he had no skills at either Basketball or volleyball, Edgar was allowed to his own privacy to hone the skills he had acquired on his tiny computer. It was during this time that he determined that his future was in his self-taught ability to wring absolutes from the Internet. Absolutes meaning that if the truth was in the computer, his skills would, excuse the pun, ferret it out.

Coveted for his skills by both the nefarious and non-nefarious organizations of the planet, he had accepted an offer from Mr. Naundorff, which made him, well, happy. Carl had a way of making people feel special. Some believed that it was the underlying belief which Carl himself never openly shared, that he was of royal blood. Others, that he had a reputation of making his people very comfortable and paying them appropriate to their own particular performance. Truth be known, his payments for failures was also legendary.

Edgar, seeing the man with the small sign reading "Wessell," steps up to him and he is courteously greeted by a jovial older hispanic man in a chauffeur's cap with a broad grin that repeats the name from the sign with the slightest of nondescript accents, "Mr. Wessell?"

Edgar nods, and the chauffeur leads him to the appropriate giant steel luggage-spitting claim area and then outside to the waiting limo parked in the exclusive VIP limo parking area. As he gets in the limo, Edgar asks in an accent-less, to-the-point question, "Wi-Fi?"

The chauffeur responds with a smile, "Yes sir, per our instructions sir."

Edgar lights up his sophisticated and highly modified

Mac Book Pro and seeks his most recent instructions from Mr. Naundorff in the form of an e-mail reading, "The company is discreet, and several of the drivers have proven very helpful in the past. They indicated that they would send Mr. Hernandez as your driver. When you get to the house, please make a list of any personal items you will require including food, and he will see to it, but only this once. Should you need anything in the information or electronic field, it would be better if you ask Demitre." Signed simply "Carl' The signature added a personal touch that mid-echelon criminals where seldom used to. He looks up momentarily and says, "Demitre?" He then opens his briefcase and pulls out a sheet of paper and pen. He taps the pen habitually on his knee and starts to write his shopping list for the driver.

As they arrive just a few miles from the airport in Venice, California, Edgar is escorted to a beautiful bungalow half a block from the beach where he is met by a familiar face, "Demitre, are you working for,..." But he is silenced as Demitre places his finger on his lips as a sign. "It is comforting to find a familiar face so far from home." He hands the list to the driver as he sets his single suitcase down.

Mr. Hernandez smiles and takes the list and glances at it before he responds, "I will be back in about two hours if that is OK, sir?"

Edgar responds, this time with a very slight French accent, "That would be fine."

As he departs, Edgar asks, "Carl's note said that he would be helpful."

"As he might, but that does not mean he needs to be involved in things he does not need to know."

"Quite right, quite right."

Then pointedly Edgar asks, "Our employer indicated that I was to ask you for 'other stuff'. Show me to my work area and tell me about the system."

"We use this bungalow because the previous owner installed a pair of CRS-3 routers , supposedly scalable to a total capacity of up to 322Tbps. At least in theory."

"Excellent! The computer?" Edgar asks as they turn the corner into his work room that the previous owner had converted. He sees the pair of matching units. "Ah."

"You should recognize the unit."

"With the security protocols?"

"Of course."

Edgar asks out of hand, "Of course. And a few additional security measures I suppose?" Demitre shrugs, "Carl gave several specific instruction about maintaining surveillance for the job but said that "you" would have the operational details and a few "projects" that I should also pay attention to."

Demitre asks with a smirk, "Do you recall the matter that

Mr. Timoshenko put you on last year?". Edgar nods and looks interested. Demitre continues, "Do you recall that someone broke into your security system and took money?"

"I was most distressed about that incident. Honestly also very impressed. I was able to find nothing."

Demitre offers, "I believe that the person responsible for that may be involved in this matter. He may not be, but,..."

Edgar's minds shifts into high gear. An innocent smile appears on his stern and unforgiving face as the excitement of an actual adventure is received. Demitre sees the expression and continues, "You should have the power with this equipment to, well, shall I say, redeem yourself."

Chapter 23

At Justin's sanctum in his basement, Haywood allows Justin to show the video on the large monitor to his eight employers. They watch Demitre's cold demeanor as he walks out of the hotel elevator and Barbara asks, "Maybe he's on TV. A lot of Hollywood people stay there."

As Justin yells, "That's it!" He hits the pause button and everyone turns to stare.

Evan asks the obvious as Justin is silent, apparently staring at a spot on the basement wall. "Earth to Justin. Did you see him on TV?"

Snapping out of his brief trance, Justin presses a button on another computer, and an index pops up on the screen. Seeing the reference he wants, he scrolls down and presses enter. Instantly, a grainy black-and-which video pops on that appears to be shot from a roof camera at a gas station. "Here he comes." A black Kawasaki ninja motorcycle with a man wearing a simple black helmet with full face screen pulls into view.

Haywood observes, "About the same size and build."

Albert asks, "Christ Haywood, it's from a weird angle, how can you tell that?" As the man pulls off his helmet and raises his cell phone to make a call.

Justin points at the man from Haywood's video and says, "See, I saw it on TV."

Haywood does a roll with his head disgusted with himself, "I don't believe it. I took a picture of Justin at a house in El Monte in the van and that very motorcycle drove past. What an idiot."

Evan asks confused, "He's a Russian?"

Robert blurts out, "No more Russians, God, ... wait! Doesn't it make sense? The dead bodies? I mean why the hell would someone try to kill us and then think they did and then kill Lloyd? Why not let him go back into a profitable business?"

Haywood, who is pacing now, shakes his head, "I don't know. I don't know."

Albert asks, confused, "So what do we have? What is going on? Do we have any directions to go except this Russian mystery man?"

Haywood stops and sits, grabbing a loose piece of paper and a pencil, "OK, we know Lloyd was a pervert. We know you guys stopped him." He writes, "We know that he was afraid when he figured out the computer blew up on its own. He's afraid of someone, for some reason." He looks around the room.

Albert asks, "What type of stuff might it be, I mean what are the options?"

Haywood pauses and then starts writing, saying what he

is writing, "Drugs, Prostitution, Gambling, Slaves, Weapons? They wouldn't burn the place down with everything in it."

They all look with a blank expression. Haywood continues, "So, what's least likely? It's probably not gambling, cause we're only 300 miles from Vegas. It's probably not prostitution because that's," he shrugs at the ladies, "pretty much a cottage industry around here. Slaves? We're in the wrong part of the world."

Albert asks the obvious question, "So you don't think it was the kiddy porn?"

"It looks for the world to me like the porn was a side thing. A messy side thing that they may have killed Lloyd for. I think he was acting all by himself, that's why he bolted and they put him in the mine field. If that's their main-line activity he stays, not runs."

Justin gets it, "Yeah and it's probably not drugs because hell, there's somebody selling whatever you want on every other street corner."

Evan jokes, "Except when you want something." Mary hits him with the back of her hand, "Ouch!"

Albert responds, "That only leaves weapons. That doesn't make any sense. Wouldn't that be in Serbia or someplace going after a Russian nuke?"

The light comes on in Justin's head, and he and Haywood lock eyes for a second. Justin speaks slowly.

"Only if they're looking to spend a hundred million dollars on a one-time event. Not if they are fighting against aircraft and tanks and armored vehicles. They want technology. The latest and greatest."

Justin points to Haywood who finishes, "And most of that stuff is made right here. Raytheon, Ardberg hire close to a million people in California to make the "next" stuff. Fullerton, Pasadena, right here!" There is silence as they look at each other.

Robert says, "Nah. Too far fetched. Nope." But everyone else is silent.

Haywood agrees, "You're right. So actually, we have no idea."

Chapter 24

Haywood is seated in the guest room at Justin's house with his head lowered into his hands thinking bitter thoughts. "Crap, crap, crap!" He pulls out his cell phone and dials a number and waits until the phone rings on the other end.

He hears a click and then, "McHugh."

"Boss. It's Haywood." knowing that the man on the other end of the phone was simultaneously agitated and interested as to why Haywood was actually calling him.

"OK, if it's worth a phone call, I'm listening."

Haywood smiles, "Sir, you know I'm a hound dog when I sniff something, and I sniffed something but can't figure it out. If I'm interfering with an ongoing investigation, I want to get out of the way. But if you had a rumor that might confirm something, well, it could be a huge thing."

"Go on."

Haywood continues, "A kiddy porn guy in LA named Lloyd Weber died in a mine field in Croatia. An attempt was made on the lives of four friends of mine but they survived. A hacker was killed in Lancaster. And I firmly believe this is all about one of the new weapons that is being developed out here. Weber's the key. He was a really fat guy and definitely not a hiker, but he died in a Croatian mine field 15 miles from Zagreb."

"Weapons? How the hell did you tie weapons into this string of coincidences?"

Haywood explains how they got to the conclusion. "At first I thought it might be conflict diamonds because their Internet came out of a Sierra Leon connection. But the diamond market in LA is way too savvy to let that slip in. Too much risk for marginal profit anymore, and they are just too professional." Haywood finishes by observing, "What we do know is that they are very well funded, willing to use deadly force and have serious technology available to them. These are serious guys, and I have eliminated virtually every other possibility."

"Maybe they are done already."

"Yes, they might be done. But they might not be." Haywood breaths deeply and closes, "Sir what I need is to go to Homeland Security and find out what someone would need to do to create a threat like what I'm talking about. I need to know what the pieces might look like. If it's crap, I can deal with that. But if it's real, it could be major."

"Let me get this right. You think that I'm going to give you an invite to the Department of Homeland Security so you can go on a fishing trip?"

Haywood smiles on his end of the phone knowing McHugh is relenting, "Well honestly, I may have worded it better."

McHugh pauses for a second and suggests, "The liaison between ATF and Homeland Security might be the one you need to deal with. He's a good guy, if a little straight-laced. His name is Oliver Trimble. He's assistant director for Los Angeles. I'd better have him call you."

"Thank you, sir. This means a lot to me."

Haywood relays the information to the group and closes, "I tell him and then we're out of it. They'll sweep in and find the problem or find out we're completely nuts, and it will be over. You guys just did something good. We should all feel proud." Haywood still has a look of uncertainty.

The group is smiling and satisfied until Evan asks, "But ...?" And the group leans in at Haywood.

"But, we're dealing with bureaucracies. So I keep a healthy dose of skepticism. That's all. Big, really big bureaucracies. But, we're moving forward. That's the key, keep the legs pumping."

Haywood looks at the group and specifically at Justin. "Justin, you may need to print out a bunch of the information and give it to me so I can see if there is anything classified, so you won't get caught up in this bureaucratic storm we just started. OK?"

Albert asks, "If it's Russians, should I call Uri and pick his brain?"

Haywood pauses and responds, "About the Demitre-Timoshenko connection? Yeah, it doesn't feel like Russians though, too subtle. Find out if he works somewhere else. He may know something or have a way to find out."

Chapter 25

Albert, having waited until morning to call Mississippi and disturb Uri, dials the phone at 6 AM California time. The phone is answered on the first ring, "Deputy Elmore."

Albert smiles broadly and says, "That's new, a Russian accent with a Mississippi twang. That's funny. How's Sally?"

Uri, under the name of Leonard Elmore, also smiles. "What did I do to deserve a call from you, Albert?" The cause for the name change is complicated. Uri, a reported terrorist, proved only to be a vengeful husband and father. The eight friends here, including Albert, had been instrumental in getting Uri, and his daughter reunited. As a result they had become close.

"We have a bit of a situation here, and I was wondering, or I should say we were wondering, what you knew about Demitre. He's showing up again in LA and may be involved in something bad."

"The truth is, I never met him, He thought he killed me, only I didn't die. I've been thinking about cutting a deal with his old boss, Milkoff. I know he's still pissed about the money he thought I took. I would love for Sally not to have all of the old times hanging over her head."

Albert responds, "He got it back."

"Yeah but he still blames me."

Albert offers, "Can I call him and tell him we took it?"

"That's a problem that you definitely don't want. Any ideas what Demitre might be up to?"

"We think it involves technology of some kind. Weapons maybe. We're pretty sure he's killing people though."

Uri considers, shrugs and responds, "I'll make the call. It's time I make a peace offering anyway."

Uri checks his watch and says to himself, "9 am in Mississippi makes it late afternoon in Moscow" Then he looks up a number and dials.

Bulletproof limos in Moscow mean pretty much the same as bulletproof limos in LA or New York. They are bulletproof for a reason, and generally the reasons are bad. Milkoff's cell phone vibrates, and he checks the number. Not recognizing the US number, he answers and simply says, "Da."

Uri answers quickly not wanting the mob boss to have to guess. "Yes Sir. This is Uri Vasilovich Boklov, I would imagine you remember who I am."

Shocked at the phone call, Milkoff recalls the chaos created by this one man stutters for a second and then composes himself, "Yes, What do you want."

"Peace between us. I sent your money back, and I need

to know that I and people around me are safe."

Milkoff inquires, "What's in it for me?"

"We let each other live. Simple as that. I do have a question about one of your employees though."

Curious Milkoff says, "Go on."

"What is Demitre doing now?"

"I don't know. He's working for some Frenchman. Why?"

"He showed up in LA and some friends of mine want to know what they should do."

"What is the saying from that "Star" movie? He's gone over to the dark side." Milkoff chuckles on the phone at his own joke.

Uri, contemplating what the dark side would be from Milkoff's perspective, "Then he is no concern of yours."

Milkoff replies coyly, "Kill him if you must," and hangs up the phone.

Uri decides what to take from the conversation and dials Albert's number.

Albert, seeing the number responds and he attempts to answer with a Russian southern accent, "So what did ya'll find out?"

Uri retorts joking, "You ask my help and then make fun of me. I don't care how big you are if I pop you in the kneecap."

Albert smiles and responds, "They already did that,

ended my career. Have you done any deep sea fishing down on the coast yet?"

"Na, Big Jim has me working around the clock here on a couple of hot cases, so we get time for playing with the kids but not much else. Demitre doesn't work for Milkoff anymore. He said he went over to the "dark side'."

Albert reflects, "That doesn't sound too ominous does it? From the Russian mob to the "dark side'."

"He's working for some French guy. Oh well, I think I made peace with Milkoff, at least I hope. He said "Kill him if you must." So he can't be too close to Demitre anymore. I don't think he was lying, but it's difficult to get that kind to speak the truth."

Chapter 26

Haywood is seated contemplating going home to see his family as his phone rings. "Hello."

"What in the holy bleeding hell did you get yourself into?"

Haywood leans back in his seat and smiles broadly at his enormous friend, "Big Jim. How'd you get those fat fingers of yours to dial the right numbers?"

"Speed dial. I just press stubborn idiot and you answer. Speaking of idiots, I'm thinking about another run to the coast for a Rubin sandwich."

"Don't be messing with my Rubin. A Rubin has pastrami and that thing you have is some weird brisket contraption."

"Maybe but it's seriously good. So, Leo told me about Albert calling. Now let me start off saying I don't approve of you hanging out with a Dallas Cowboy, retired or not."

"Jesus, Jim, you great big football jocks are all alike. I actually thought he was you until I found out he was black."

"How long did that take, a week? Seriously, are you messing with the Russians again?"

Haywood contemplates what he is willing to share with his friend and starts, "I think it's all wrapped up. I'm talking to some stiff-assed yankee from Homeland Security tomorrow to hand it all off. I could use ya'll to soften him up some."

"Don't you be acting like you're from the south and taking on airs. You spent enough time in New York to be classified as the enemy. Leo told me that Russian guy authorized killing one of his men. What's up with that?"

Knowing that Big Jim was much brighter and more receptive than he usually let on, he partially opened up to his friend. "We know we stirred something up but we're not sure what it is. Nothing else seems to make sense, that old Occam's Razor thing about when you eliminate what it can't be, it's generally what's left. And what's left, unless we missed something, is technology and weapons."

Big Jim pauses and adds, "Wow. Scary. You know, interestingly enough, I was reading about a mini bomb with upgraded targeting that could be shot from a two-man shoulder-launch unit that is capable of defeating almost all countermeasures. In theory, it could take out Air Force One. Scary. You need anything from us rednecks?"

"Like I said, we're turning this all over to Homeland Security tomorrow, and I go back to my wife."

"You mean, Ex wife!"

"I'm working on her. Heck, the kids are working on her too." Haywood multitasks his cell phone and texts the picture of his grandson Mike with the fish to Big Jim. "I'm sending you a picture if you can receive text messages down there in hill-billy country."

Big Jim opens the file and smiles at his phone, "Is that your bait?"

"No that's Mike."

"I meant the fish, shit head."

"I went to a place where I didn't think we would be disturbed by man or beast, and that slimy, scaly thing Mike's holding grabbed onto his fishhook and interfered with our beer drinking."

Still not completely satisfied, Big Jim continues, "Haywood, you turn this thing over to someone and find an excuse to come visit. Bring that pup Mike with you and I'll show you some real fishin. In fact, my anniversary is next week. I think Billy Kilmer is coming down."

"You just saying that."

"No I'm not. I saved his life every week for four years and he likes my wife's cooking. Don't tell him I'm gonna do all the cooking though, he just remembers me burning the piss out of everything."

"The temptation is great, but I still have to make a living. I can't get my full retirement for another two years. So I probably will head back to the family. I will plan coming down and show you how to fish though. Say hi to Uri."

"I hope you change your mind."

After they hang up, Big Jim calls Leo into his office. "Come on in son, Haywood says Hi. I have a feeling your

---

friends are into something they may have some trouble with. How you you feel about some LAPD joint task force terrorist training?"

Leo is slightly concerned about his friends in Malibu and asks with the slightest Russian Accent, "Do you really think they're in some trouble?"

Big Jim leans back and contemplates, "I don't know. What I do know is one of my friends may need some help and I want to have boots on the ground if it comes to trouble."

Leo, still troubled by the name change, is fortunate to live in a place where everyone knows him by his new name so the only confusion is his own. "I'm in. I have to make arrangements about Sally."

"Don't hurry, I think we have some time still."

Chapter 27

Seated in the outer office of the assistant director of Homeland Security for the entire western coast of the United States, Haywood continues to mull over exactly what he knows to be true and what he can legitimately tell without getting his friends into trouble. Finally selecting his plan of attack, he is called to the inner office, where a stern-looking thin balding man looks up from his stack of work and stands. Oliver Trimble's face changed, assuming a "genuine" and practiced smile designed and rehearsed with the express purpose of putting people at ease. Being a product of a massive bureaucracy, it has the exact opposite effect on Haywood. Having battled bureaucracy for a good portion of his adult life in the FBI, he sets aside his inner-most anxiety and reaches to shake the man's hand.

"First, I need to express my gratitude for being heard. I'm sure you've seen my work record at the FBI, and I will admit that I was not always a team player. But when I got the scent of something, my instincts were pretty good. I have the scent of something that may be a huge problem, and I have no authority to do anything except express my deep concerns and turn it over to someone that can look into it. The details are in the file I sent. I assume you went through that and have some questions."

Assistant Director of Homeland Security Oliver Trimble points to a chair for Haywood and sits in the matching overstuffed chair right next to Haywood. He assumes his most genuine expression, reserved for Television and grieving widows, looks deep into Haywood's eyes and starts, "Your supervisor, Special Agent McHugh said you were trouble, but that you did have good instincts. Those instincts were right on too. Mr. Haywood, although I appreciate your concern, we have this matter under investigation currently and it is totally under our control. The manner through which you appear to have discovered this information aside, you can be assured that the Office of Homeland Security has the situation well in hand and we are currently wrapping up our investigation." He waits for Haywood to acknowledge and Haywood nods. "As you are aware, it is vital that you stay out of the way of this vast and expensive investigation." He stands and grabs his expensive suit jacket and motions toward the door. "If you would be so kind as to walk with me to the elevator, I am in fact on my way to be briefed on this ongoing investigation. Unfortunately, as you are no longer with the FBI, I'm afraid I won't be able to share any of our findings with you. To be honest, this is exactly the type of thing we try to keep out of the news until we have the facts straight." He smiles as if sharing a secret and winks at Haywood, "In fact, I'm afraid

I've probably told you too much already."

Haywood, knowing a "bums rush" when he sees it, stands and smiles, forcing the bile that is effectively building in his system to settle briefly and says as cordially as he can. "Mr. Trimble, I realize I'm not bringing much to the table except for a conspiracy theory and a spotty record, but I believe this is real. I would genuinely appreciate knowing that this isn't going to end here."

Aware that his bullshit story may have been seen through, Trimble opens the door to the outer office and becomes less cordial. "Mr. Haywood, I have attempted to be gracious as a courtesy to a retired colleague. Don't press your luck. You know that becoming involved in our investigation is a felony." He closes his door and walks past Haywood out of the outer office and toward the elevator.

At the ground floor, Trimble dials his cell phone as he gets into his car. Without a word to the driver, the vehicle pulls from the curb and is off.

Seated at his desk working as always on his computer, Carl is startled slightly as his phone rings. He picks up the phone and checks the number. Slightly perturbed by the intrusion, he answers curtly, "We have a protocol, Oliver. You need to follow the protocol."

"Yes sir. A retired FBI Agent was in my office with some rather startling information about the plan. I felt it was important to advise you that it might be best if we delayed and let this settled. I think I chased him away. Let it settle."

"Was his name Haywood?"

Startled, Trimble says, "Why yes."

"Obviously we are aware of the situation, so please, when I ask you to follow certain rules or suffer the consequences, understand that I am serious." Carl hangs up the phone.

Trimble is upset and says loud enough for the driver to hear, "Who does he think I am to talk to me like that!"

Carl checks the time and calls Demitre, "Yes sir."

Carl starts, "Demitre, it is time to sidetrack Haywood. Do not kill him. But destroy his credibility. A dead investigator can be worse than a live one. They will close the investigation once that is done."

Chapter 28

The Tacoma Police station is busier than a non-resident might suspect. The recently promoted chief of investigations, Kathleen Kincaid, is a zealot about kids and drugs. Anything that leads to the potential drug abuse of children gets a high priority for all purposes in her book, an honorable and trustworthy book for anyone that is a parent. The call that came in at 5 AM was about the worst kind of drugs. Oxycodone hydrochloride, a synthetic form of heroin, is an amazingly expensive pharmaceutical and is the drug of choice for young adults. The dilemma, as with all opiates, is once addicted, the need exceed, the ability to pay. Therefore, logically, heroin, which is available and much cheaper becomes the drug of convenience. The phone call mentioning oxycodone hydrochloride was taken seriously. In fact, too seriously, which is one of the drawbacks of being a zealot. The knee-jerk tendency is to react quickly and with maximum force.

At Haywood's humble home, the questionable warrant was sufficient to allow his door to be broken open, the house ransacked and the planted drugs easily located. The credibility of the phone call from the anonymous witness that refused to leave his name was enough to crush the spirit of the dedicated chief of investigations when the assistant District Attorney rained on her celebratory parade. Heated words were exchanged and Haywood's license to carry a gun and Investigate in the State of Washington were revoked subject to review. All before he was even given a simple phone call.

The first actual notification that Haywood had that any of this was going on was a discreet phone call from a retired associate from Haywood's days on the Tacoma PD. The second, was the spread in virtually every newspaper in the USA. Headlines reading, EX FBI AGENT ARRESTED FOR DRUGS with the same picture that made the national press from a murder near a military base the year before. This time, cropped down to show only Haywood in his wrinkled jacket and that exhausted look.

Haywood, reeling from the body blow, sees the number and picks up the phone on the first ring. Instead of the normal salutations, he opens with, "You know I didn't have anything to do with that."

McHugh sighs before answering, "It's a hard sell, that 'someone else' put ten thousand dollars worth of drugs in my house. But, ..." He trails off.

Haywood responds pleadingly, "At least tell me you know I didn't do it."

"And what good does my word do?"

"To me, the world." Haywood waits for his answer patiently.

"Then you have it. I've already offered to speak at the retirement hearing. That's why I'm calling. They want you to come to Washington DC for a hearing about your retirement. Someone wants to take it away. It's not scheduled for two months, they want to do a thorough investigation."

It's Haywood's turn to sigh deeply, "Then I'm good. You know I don't care what they do as long as the people that know me believe in me."

"You'd better care. The conspiracy theory alibi gets no play around DC these days -- you are in a pile of shit with no friends."

Haywood pauses, "You believe me. That's a start." They disconnect.

Haywood's phone rings with a friendly number and he sighs and answers, "Hey Big, how ya doing?"

"You're a real popular asshole aren't you. Get a shipment of drugs and don't share them with a friend?"

"Not a thing to joke about Big Jim. I'm guessing you should say hi to the FBI doing the internal investigation trying to take my retirement away who are probably listening in."

"They can't believe it, can they?"

"Jim they have to take it seriously, I understand that. I'm

finished though, my credibility was pretty much my only real asset, and nobody wants to get close to me now."

"You have a lot of friends, Haywood. You're not alone. Talk to your wife and then come down here till it cools off. Still a couple days till my party."

Haywood, seriously considering the offer, responds, "OK, let me call and square it with the ex. The last time we talked she was OK, but I don't know if she'd want to go with me."

"She believes they're not your drugs, right?"

Haywood hesitates for a second, "Yeah, it's not that. It's hard to take the attention from the media, and it's way simpler to say "we've been separated for ten years'."

"Call her and bring her down."

Chapter 29

By the time Haywood is at Evan's beach house, his eight employers, have worked themselves into a fit of anger. Justin starts right in before Haywood can get seated, "So they at least have someone in Homeland Security, someone at Customs and at one of the plants, either Raytheon or Ardberg. I'm running a crunch to see any that may have anything in common,..."

Haywood holds up his hand and interrupts and says, "I'm done. I have no credibility, and you're done too. You guys stopped a kiddy porn distributor and worse. Be proud and let it go. Whoever it is, is way over your heads."

They all protest. Evelyn is the loudest, "You can't give up! Someone ruined your life!"

Haywood persists, "No, they didn't do anything to me that I can't live with. You know the truth and I will eventually be cleared. But we're done. We have no leads, I can't ask anyone on the inside anymore. Demitre checked out of his hotel, and they certainly aren't going to give me any forwarding address. What do we do." They protest, and he continues, "I'm going home and then to Mississippi for a few weeks to drink beer and talk football with some real men." They finally all smile and acknowledge that he is leaving.

Justin hands Haywood a credit card and says, "Just in case you find something, we want you on the clock."

Haywood takes the card and says, "I'm using it to go to Mississippi, I'm going to ask Margaret to go. Oh, there's a party at Big Jim's house for his anniversary. Anyone interested?"

Albert offers, "Really? Barbara needs a break and I want to see if I can knock his big ass down, so we're in." Barbara shrugs and nods approval.

Evelyn smiles, "We can't go. Sorry, but I calculated the hours you were here and sent your payment directly into your business account. So you have some cash for the trip."

Haywood responds, "Thanks. Now please, if you find something out, don't put yourselves at risk on this. If something comes up, let me know."

Haywood starts packing and then sits on his bed and dials the phone, truly scared about the phone call. "Margaret?"

His ex-wife asks, "Haywood, are you OK?"

He relaxes when he hears her tone and says, "I'm so sorry about all this, I've called to ask you something."

She sits down and starts, "Look, I know you didn't do anything with drugs. That was stupid. They set up Mister Perfect and didn't realize who they were trying to set up."

Reacting to a hurt silence on the other end of the line, she continues, "I don't mean anything by the Mister Perfect comment, Haywood, you are who you are, that's all. Tell me what you want."

"I've been invited to a party in Mississippi, and I would really like for you to come with me. No strings attached. Separate rooms, whatever. I just want you to meet my friends and have a good time. They're great people."

"You think you might get lucky?" After an awkward second, she continues, "Well, you might, so what's the weather going to be like?"

"It's Mississippi, so hot and humid. Warm evenings with lightning bugs and children chasing them with jars. The smell of jasmine in the air. Honestly, if I didn't want to stay close to you and the kids, I'd move."

"What's a girl to wear?"

Milkoff, seated in his office sipping coffee from a tiny china cup is weighing options on a difficult choice. Finally, he sets the cup down and dials an international number on his cell phone.

Carl, seated in his limo just leaving the government offices in Paris checks the number and responds flatly, unsure of who exactly is calling. "Hello."

Milkoff responds, "Yes, this is Milkoff from Moscow. Do you know who I am?"

Carl, slightly in shock from the call from a Russian mob boss responds, "Yes, I know who you are. How can I assist you?"

"I would like a trade. I need something handled and I will trade something you will be interested in, I believe."

"I'm afraid I don't understand what you are saying sir."

"Let's just say that it involves our mutual friend Demitre. A job he failed at once, I need him to finish. In exchange, I will offer you something."

"It would depend on what the information is."

"Yes, of course. The person I want dealt with called me to find out who Demitre was working for now, to find out what he was involved with. I told him I know nothing."

Carl reflects silently for a few seconds before responding, "Done. Where would he locate this old comrade?"

"May I text you the information?"

"Certainly."

Chapter 30

Demitre wakes as dawn breaks to the sound of a text being received on his cell phone and sits up in bed to check. The hotel room in the morning light is not nearly as well appointed as the one in Santa Monica, but Demitre had moved simply because his instincts had said to move and his instincts were seldom wrong. Seeing the text, he is momentarily confused and then shakes his head cursing out loud. "Uri." The text carefully spells out where he can be located and the specific instructions that he should not go himself.

Checking the time, he lays back down for a few seconds as if to recapture his sleep and then sits up resigned and dials his phone. In Russian he speaks as the phone is answered, "Pavel, my friend, I have an acquaintance I need for you to say "hi" to, as quickly and as loudly as possible. I will send you the details. Don't call me with questions until the team is assembled and you are on the way." Listening, he answers, "Yes, now!" He clicks off the phone and lays back down knowing he will never get back to sleep. He opens his eyes and again says bitterly, "Uri!"

Cursing, Demitre sits up, tosses his legs over the edge of the bed and rubs the sleep from his eyes. All the time contemplating how someone he had killed less than 12 months before had risen from the dead. Ruminating on how many people had died believing that they too had killed the same man. The undying Uri. Now it was again his job to conclude his life. Standing and stretching, Demitre walks to the bathroom and turns on the shower. Cursing, "Uri."

Chapter 31

At the airport as Albert and Barbara walk off the plane with Haywood and Margaret in the lead, they all gawk at the near 7-foot giant waiting at the gate with a big grin and open arms. Haywood walks up and the embrace looks like a man hugging a small child as Haywood turns and says, "Margaret, this is Big Jim. Don't get in his way when he's eating, it could be dangerous!"

Big jim gently hugs the petite woman and she shakes her head and says, "He said you were big but I was not ready for this."

Big Jim, with a wink and a smile, responds, "Think of me as your favorite giant teddybear." Big Jim looks sourly at Albert, and the slight scent of ozone can be smelled with the feeling that sparks are about to fly. He says, "I hate the Cowboys!"

Albert grins broadly and offers his hand and say, "Me too." Big Jim 5 inches and 50 pounds bigger, but inches narrower through the shoulders, slides past the offered hand and hugs Albert firmly. The hug is returned in kind, and the seed of true friendship is planted.

Bug Jim says with a wink, "People in all 9 southern states hate the Redskins because they represent

Washington DC and the Union. So me playing for the enemy was complicated. You, should do fine. There a bunch of idiots that like the Dallas Cowboys here about."

Albert, smiles and leans in, "I saw you play, and I know how good you really were."

Big Jim leans in and responds in a near whisper, "I saw you play and know you were better, but I appreciate the thought."

Arm in arm the big men walk toward the exit and they stop on the street as Big Jim opens the rear doors to his squad car. "Albert, I'm afraid you're going to have to sit up here with me."

Albert responds coyly, "Don't be afraid." as the other three crawling into the back of the vehicle laugh.

Haywood asks, "Are we going to have to deal with this macho shit the whole time?"

Big Jim's house is a postcard of the south. A huge two-story house painted white with big windows and a patio that reaches almost the entire way around the house. By the time the squad car pulls in, they are all best friends and Margaret is holding Haywood's hand affectionately, truly enjoying the camaraderie. She offers, "Haywood said it would be hot and humid. But this evening is perfect. Except he promised me lightning bugs."

Big Jim apologizes, "They're unpredictable, but they'll

show up."

As the car stops Haywood runs to hug Jim's wife, Wilma, and it still looks odd because she is six inches taller than him. He shakes hands with Jim Junior and says, "I have missed you guys," as the rest gather and wait for introductions. Big Jim is left to the introductions, and they find chairs on the enormous porch. The women find their way to the kitchen and bring plates of home cooked-food to the men.

Big Jim asks his wife, "Are we going to be able to count on this domesticated wife stuff for a while?"

She kicks his chair and says, "As soon as they leave, we go back to you serving me!" and everyone laughs as the women sit down and they all eat.

In the near darkness of late dusk, under a lone street light at the end of the long shrub-lined driveway, a squad car driven by Uri, with Sally beside him, pulls in and moves slowly toward the house. Discreetly behind it, a black Suburban SUV pulls up at the end of the driveway and stops, blocking the drive. Albert and Big Jim, sensing danger, move first pushing the women into the house, and Big Jim runs faster than a man that size should be able to, into his den to unlock the gun safe. Uri, without realizing his dilemma, steps out of the squad car just as the man in the front seat of the SUV opens up on him full automatic with the unmistakable roar of the Israeli Uzi in his hand. Uri pitches forward on the ground after the first volley as the other three in the SUV open up on the squad car. Sally flattens out of view on the car seat frightened and screaming at the destruction around her.

Haywood, for the first time in years without a gun, refuses to take safety and is standing stationary on the porch as Jim returns to the porch holding two automatic weapons. The first he flips to Haywood and the second he sets on his shoulder and they both lay down a heavy barrage of cover fire as the four men, shocked that they are getting return fire, move their aim to the porch. Two from the SUV are clipped quickly and fall with indeterminate injuries as the driver gets in the SUV and they load their wounded and flee. Automatic fire follows them the short distance to the edge of the trees as they speed off, riddling the SUV and knocking out the rear and back side windows. Jim grabs his walkie talkie which, he was wearing the entire time, and calls for backup as Barbara and Haywood run to Uri's unmoving form. Sally is still screaming in panic and jumps out of the riddled squad car and runs to her father. Haywood grabs Sally and says, "Sweetie, your dad's in good hands, let her work." She sobs but stands and hugs Haywood still screaming and crying out of control.

Barbara presses on a bad hole in Uri's back as he winces and looks up at her saying, "I just wanted to say hi," and passes out.

With a tear in her eye, Barbara steels herself and preforms a battlefield exam and sighs a huge sigh of relief. "He took three rounds but nothing vital, I think. I hope. Is the ambulance coming?"

Haywood looks at Albert with a quizzical expression, "Is this from the call to Milkoff?"

Albert realizes with a shock, "This is my fault?"

Barbara sees the pitiful look on Albert's face and yells him into action. "Albert, get over here and apply pressure on these wounds." He snaps to and runs to help.

Chapter 32

Later in the waiting room of the hospital, Barbara is bouncing off the wall, unused to being in a hospital and not in action. Finally, she darts out of the room mid-anxiety attack. Jim, Albert and Haywood are huddled. Jim asks, "Did you see that Demitre fellow?"

Albert and Haywood glance at each other and Albert responds, "No. Definitely not. He's taller than those guys. Does that mean there are two groups?"

Haywood responds first, "No but it may mean Milkoff is involved somehow. They weren't expecting return fire. They didn't know who you are Jim, so they are not local."

Jim considers the facts, "Did you tell your friends in LA? They could be targets too?"

Albert nods and says, "It was Uri they were after, they may have seem me, but they weren't looking at me. They were more concerned about the giant and the little guy, and the what the hell were those rifles you guys shooting?"

Big Jim blushes and responds, "Sir, I'm afraid I have no idea what you're talking about." Albert looks at Haywood who winks back at him. Albert shrugs and says, "Well I know what I want for Christmas."

Jim asks, "Can you shoot?"

Albert shrugs again, "Barbara hates guns, but yeah, I can shoot. Not like Haywood there, buy I can hit a target."

Big Jim looks at Haywood, and Haywood responds, "Justin's a bit shaky under fire, wanting to stand up and make a target, but the other three can lay down a pattern just fine. And they pulled Uri out of the frying pan once already."

Albert says, "With help."

Jim nods approvingly. "Alright then. Those were the new-issue Israeli combat weapons, the shoulder-model Uzi. I'd put it in the HK class. And I only have two, but I got some other stuff I could'a brought out, but I,..."

Haywood interrupts, "Albert. It's a red neck and his guns. Deal with it."

Albert stifles a laugh and says, "That didn't keep him from giving you one."

Big Jim leans in closer and says, "On our first run to the coast... "

Haywood interrupts, "For a Rubin sandwich, where we got stopped and yelled at 'cause we were in a squad car, lights and siren, in someone else's territory."

Jim looks shocked, "It was an emergency! How can you say that?"

Haywood acknowledges, "It was a pretty good sandwich. Tell the story."

"Anyway. They sicked the sheriff on us, and after we

butted heads, he'd heard about Haywood and that thing in LA, so we went shooting. Haywood is dead nuts with a pistol, pretty good with a rifle, but unreal with automatic weapons."

Albert looks at Haywood, "I've seen him in action. But I didn't know he was special."

Haywood shakes his head and responds, "Guys the guns were made by people my size and strength. They track in a certain way. It's a dance. You pull the trigger and let the thing work."

Albert looks at Big Jim, and Jim says, "He tried telling us this crap at the gun range in Gulf Port too. It's total shit!" And the three chuckle as a very stern Barbara with Margaret in tow walks into the room and scowls at them.

Barbara settles down, and Margaret sits next to Haywood and takes his hand in hers. Barbara speaks as if involved in their previous conversation, "So the way I see it, they would need someone actually in the manufacturing plant, either logistics or, well, just in shipping. But they would need someone in either customs or Homeland Security or both."

Haywood responds, "*and* a ton of money to throw at it. We have Justin looking for anything, any connection at all. It's a big field, though and it will take a while."

Barbara responds, "We don't have a while. They're shooting my friends. Oh god where is Sally?"

Big Jim hugs Barbara and says, "She lost it, but she was so glad you were there. She didn't care about anything else, but you saved him last time, so she was sure you would do it again. She's a tough girl."

Barbara sighs with a tear in her eye, "Whose had a pretty rough year."

Jim hugs tighter, "Yes she has."

Chapter 33

Justin is having lunch with Evelyn in the kitchen sipping a Coke Zero and nibbling on a BLT when a ring, like a cheap timer goes, off and Evelyn asks, "Are you doing laundry?"

"No, my big search may have found something. That's the ring of inspiration."

She shakes her head and says, "What a nerd! What the hell am I doing with a nerd?"

He stands and kisses her on the forehead and says, "I ask myself the same thing every day. Trust me," and walks toward the stairs to his lair.

He flips through the notes that have been printed off and dials Albert on his cell phone. "Albert, your sister in law called me a nerd."

Albert responds, "You are. Deal with it. Uri, I mean Leo, is OK. Had to patch and re-inflate a lung. Shattered bone in his arm, and a through and through in his other arm. From the stories I've heard, though, he's used most of his nine lives."

He flips to speaker phone as Justin replies, "Not much to report from the computer. The asshole Haywood met with at Homeland was at the same place in France as the senator that is behind the railroading of Haywood."

"What senator."

Justin replies, "Senator Carter was the one that wanted Haywood in a retirement hearing. You guys didn't know that. He even went on TV."

Albert offers, "Uri said that Demitre was working for a Frenchman. You don't think..."

Barbara adds, "No such thing as a coincidence, right. So what can you tell us about the French guy?"

"They went to the same place. That's all. Wait, you think this is the like the same French guy?" Silence on the phone before Justin answers, "OK, I'll see."

Big Jim's look is severe and concerned, "What are you going to do?"

Haywood drops his head. "I guess I'm back in. I wanted to spend some time with Margaret," he looks at he as he finishes, "but, like Barbara says, They're shooting at my friends."

Margaret asks, "What can I do to help? Don't use me as an excuse. I'll wait for you if you want me to." She leans toward him and they kiss.

"Then I need you to be safe so we can figure out what's going on. We're going back to Malibu and get to the bottom of this, and I don't even have a place for you to stay."

Albert and Barbara speak at the same time, Barbara

being the loudest, "We have servant quarters, can you cook?"

Margaret looks at her, confused, as Haywood and Albert start to laugh. Barbara smiles and says, "I'm sorry, that wasn't fair. You know I'm kidding, right?"

Margaret has a concerned smile and Barbara takes her hands. "I'm never home, and Albert will be with Haywood, so you'll need a car. We have a 5-year-old Camry that you can drive. We would love to have you."

Margaret smiles and responds, "I'm a pretty good cook, too."They all smile as Margaret hugs Barbara.

Uri's doctor walks in and Barbara grabs him by the lapels of his smock, and Albert intervenes and pries her away. "Jesus, Barb. Let him breath."

The doctor straightens himself and says, I'll be fine and so will Uri. I noticed a bunch of other scarring that looked like bullet wounds and a nasty scar between his eyes,... "The doctor trails off.

Haywood replies, "Like a friend of mine just said. If he had nine lives he's used most of them."

The doctor looked at Big Jim and asks without asking. "Sheriff?"

Big Jim shrugs and says, "Do what you need to do, doc. File whatever you need to. You don't have to report what happened years ago. He was involved in a fire fight last night and he's fine. I would like to know if you hear about any other bullet wounds around the county, or maybe a doctor that doesn't show up for work."

The doctor acts shocked by the question and says, "Well Dr. Tanaka was supposed to be here at midnight and,..."

Big Jim interrupts to ask, "Do you know his address?"

Barbara responds for the doctor, "Go, I'll call you from Admin," as the three men run for the door.

Barbara says as they disappear around the corner, "They still want Uri."

The doctor asks, "I thought his name was Leonard?" as Haywood stops mid stride.

Haywood says, "I don't think you'll find them, and if they come here, I'll be dressed in a smock and acting like I'm trying to catch 40 winks."

Big Jim grabs Albert by the arm and as they run down the hall he yells back saying, "By the authority vested in me by Rankin County Mississippi, I do hereby Deputize you Samuel Haywood."

Haywood yells as they run out the door, "I want to talk about benefits!" Then turns to Barbara. "Can you find me a smock?"

Barbara says, "I saw two of them go down in the fire fight."

Haywood responds, "One center mass and one not. The center mass is probably OK with a bruise because of body armor, the other one is probably out of commission. I'm surprised that no one has seen that Suburban with the bullet holes though."

Chapter 34

Justin is wide awake in his sanctum securum, a mug of piping hot coffee in his grasp and several empty mugs nearby. On his screen he has an image of Carl's amazing house and his row of printers are belching out product at their maximum pace. Evelyn walks down the stairs with a plate of eggs and toast and asks, "Are you going to sleep?"

Justin looks up, "We should have been there with them, sweetie pie."

Evelyn sets the food down and hugs him as he works and says, "Do you honestly think you would have been more valuable there, instead of here?"

He cocks his head sideways and turns to kiss her. "You are my miracle, that you put up with me for all these years."

"Stupid! You're filthy rich. I would have married a goat with that kind of money."

Justin sits up shocked, "That's the question I didn't ask. Dumb dumb, dumb." and starts typing.

Evelyn touches his face as she walks out and says, "About a goat? Eat while it's warm sweetie."

Justin takes his fork and scoops a large mouthful and turns back to the computer without apparently missing a stroke on the keyboard. Then he says with a full mouth,

"Thank you, my love. Not the goat, the money!" and she walks up the stairs.

Outside of a small rental home in midtown, that appropriately reflects the economic status of an intern in Rankin County, Albert and Big Jim are at the door with three cars filled with backup. There are no lights on anywhere in the house.

Big Jim, with body armor large enough for a small car, pounds on the door yelling, "Sheriff's Office, open the door." After 20 seconds of silence, with several lights coming on in the small neighborhood around them, he yells again, "Sheriff's Office, open the door or we will knock it down." This is followed by more silence except the neighbor's door opening and a deputy telling the occupant to go inside and lock his door.

Albert offers, "I always wanted to knock a door down, Big Jim."

Big Jim responds, "I'm afraid of your wife, Albert, so forget it." He raises his leg and kicks the door with his full body weight, and the hinges groan and give up as the door falls inside off the hinges with a crash.

The deputies swarm the house, and one reports from the bathroom, "Two bodies here."

Big Jim and Albert stand at the door to the bathroom peering in to see an Asian man in pajamas with a gun shot to the back of his head and one man in the bathtub with a neck wound that bled, out still partly dressed in the same body armor as those that attacked Uri.

Albert's phone rings, and he sees Justin's cell number and answers, "What the hell are you doing up, asshole."

Justin laughs into the phone, "Screw you too, tons of fun."

"I got a hit and a note. First, a Gulf Stream flew into a private airport last night with four passengers and left three hours ago with three. Anybody you know?"

"Yes it fits. Where did they go? LA?"

"Vegas. Our boy in France has a name, Carl Wilhelm Naundorff de Bourbon XII."

"Royalty?"

"Wanna be royalty maybe. Carl Wilhelm Naundorff, the First, claimed to be the first born son of Louis XIV and heir to the Bourbon throne of France. Only, he had to buy the "de Bourbon" part from the Dutch Government. I mean, why wouldn't they allow him to change names for some cash?" Justin shuffles some papers and continues, "Got partly derailed with the advent of DNA in 1990 or so. That doesn't stop him from making a claim. Lives in a castle in the south of France. Which is how I found him. Seems to like politicians and scum bags. Can't follow his money out, but tried to follow the money in, and it reeks of ill-gotten gains."

"You think it's him then?"

"Yeah, ..."

"But?"

"I'd feel better if I could prove it. Then we would have some leverage over that senator to get off Haywood's back."

Chapter 35

Carl is livid. He stands from his desk and paces with the cell phone, unable to speak. He repeatedly tenses his fist raised in front of his chest in a vain effort to control the bile rising in his stomach. First the audacity of that Russian pig to presume to ask for a favor, and then, he slams his fist on the desk hurting his own hand with the force -- then the stupidity of me agreeing to the favor. "Demitre, you have no choice but to finish the job. I did not give you a job to fail."

"Sir, I was instructed not to go."

"I am supposed to know you will send idiots to do this job?" Contemplating his timetable he asks, "Now, will we have enough time to complete the job before we have to complete the shipment?"

"Sir, I told you not to deal with,..."

Interrupting, Carl spews angrily, "Do you presume to lecture me? You work for me because you have experienced men at your disposal. How many can you get? Tell me quickly!"

"As I said, sir, anywhere in the world in two days I can get between four and twelve men. More is longer. Same as before."

Carl settles down and contemplates his options slowly

before he speaks, "What does Milkoff know?"

"He will know they missed."

"Merd! You have placed me in a difficult place. You must decide how to get me out. Do you have any suggestions?"

"Sir, getting Uri is important only to Milkoff. Let him wait until the job is done and then we can send everyone after him if you want."

Carl contemplates his options and responds, "Yes, You will take care of the shipment first. I will let you know what to do about the other." He clicks off the phone and says, "Merd!" He then dials a number from his speed dial and when answered says, "You and three men to Mississippi now. I will give you instructions on the way. I sent a hammer to do a quiet job, and the hammer missed the nail. Do nothing if you cannot complete the job. I'll have a plane waiting in New York. Then, when you are finished, I need you in Los Angeles." He clicks off again and again says, "Merd!" and massages his injured hand.

In Cape Town, South Africa, three fair-skinned but tanned men of similar size and weight enter a bar on the Air France terminal at the airport. A fourth man, a few inches shorter and a few years older, signals them over and speaks to them in "Afrikaner," which is a combination of Dutch, German and the local African dialect. They are traveling light as the seated man greets them, "Good to see you. We have 20 minutes until we board. We will be gone at least two weeks, maybe more. Any questions?"

They all nod. One with a shaved head smiles and winks at the seated man before they all sit near him, "Good to see you, Malcolm, me brothers and me were getting a bit bored. Can't shoot the kaffers anymore, they'll lock you up. Shooting at targets gets boring. What are we off to?"

Malcolm answers in English but with an Australian accent, "Not like the old days, eh mate. I can't promise you anything except action. We're supposed to be in stealth mode here. Then off to Los Angeles for some proper shooting."

The three men smile cruelly and order drinks before departure. The man on the end adds as he sips his beer, "I heard they have some really big kaffers in America, I want to shoot me one of them."

Chapter 36

Justin is sorting through paperwork and vents to himself in the empty room, "Aargh. What am I doing?" He checks the time and dials his phone. Robert answers and Justin says, "I need you guys over here. OK?"

Twenty minutes later, Robert and Evan wander down the stairs to Justin's basement workshop. Both are clean shaven and fresh faced next to Justin's disheveled and completely burned-out look. Bleary eyed, Justin says, "I'm on to something and I think we need it quickly, but I'm shot. Please look through this stuff and see what we have." He points at a stack of papers a foot high and then at a second stack a few pages high. "The details are here. The guy's name, bank accounts, visitors, who they work for when I could find it, he has a Gulf Stream I'm tracking, but I need two hours of sleep, and I won't be able to if you guys aren't at least trying to help."

Evan says, "Cool. We're on it."

Justin looks at Robert, "Dude, you need to look through he business stuff and see if there is anything we can learn. I hit that stuff and it turns to jelly in my brain. Useless."

Robert grabs a stack and responds, "Sure, whatever I can do."

Evan picks up the short stack and jokes, "I'll do this one," as Robert ignores him.

Justin stands and says, "I'll be back in a couple hours. If you find something, call Haywood and Albert, OK?"

With his vast background in business and management, Robert starts slowly and then starts to engage the business acumen lying dormant in the back of his mind. The focus starts to return, and he sorts and sorts through the stacks of documents about Carl's mysterious world.

Later, as Justin comes back down the stairs with a cup of coffee, Evan is asleep in his chair with his head tilted back and his mouth open snoring softly. Robert now has the large stack sorted into five smaller stacks with overlapping ends and little yellow sticky notes on the edges of the documents to show what they are. Robert speaks as Justin looks on impressed, "Just in time. How do you feel? You looked like you were in a zombie movie when you left."

"Two hours sleep and a shower, and I'm a new man. What did you find?"

He tosses a pencil at Evan which startles him and almost knocks him backwards off the chair. Evan yells, "I'm awake! What?"

Robert smiles and shrugs, "Something. If we could access the Swiss accounts, we would have the answers, but I'll assume you can't so I'll show you what we know." He points to the first stack. "This is a transfer from a Swiss account, which we don't know who owns or controls to purchase a Gulf Stream, cash! Used but perfect, like three or four thousand miles. Then the same account sends money to the Cayman's to an account, which transfers money to an account owned by this guy, Rodney Jenkins, at Ardberg. Barbara guessed it, he's in something called Distribution and Transportation Logistics services. She said "shipping," but that's what they call it now. Then this Jenkins goof pays off his house. Bad move, actually. If I was the guy that set this up, he would be with the laundry when the delivery is finished cause he's busted. The good news for Mr. de Bourbon is, the trail stops at the Swiss account. So unless he attaches his corporate emblem to the side of that Gulf Stream, he's clean. Now another transfer from the same Swiss account goes into a different Cayman account the same day that Oliver Trimble visits the South of France. Coincidence? Then the afternoon that Haywood goes to Homeland Security to talk to Trimble, he calls an unlisted cell phone in France to a cell tower in the south of France which services Mr. de Bourbon's villa, castle, whatever. Sweet house by the way." He pauses for effect, "Then the coupe de gras, the good Senator Carter, doing his civic duty in calling Haywood to the carpet for his indiscretion, calls the FBI before the news hits the streets. So I ask, how exactly did he work up his civic indignation for the vile and repugnant act of our Mr. Haywood when he can't possibly know about it yet?"

Justin is impressed, "You got all of that from that stack of shit?"

"It's called timing. The key, put it into order and sort relevance. Then, viola, the shit falls into place."

Evan adds, "You should'a been a lawyer."

Robert looks at Evan with acid in his eyes, "I hate lawyers, don't even joke."

Justin adds, "Dude, you even sound like one. You're becoming what you hate!"

"Are you guys trying to make me sick?"

They both nod yes.

Chapter 37

Albert tosses in his fitful sleep next to Barbara, and she wakes up and snuggles waking him up. He roles over, and they hug and Barbara asks seriously, "What are we going to do?"

Albert shakes his head and answers, "I don't know. I'll tell you, I really like having these two around though."

Barbara smiles, knowing he is referring to Big Jim and Haywood and says, "Mutt and Jeff?"

Albert fights back a laugh and asks, "So which one was the big one? Mutt or Jeff?"

She giggles, and they hear dishes being set in the kitchen. Barbara kisses him on the forehead, "I have to go help. They think I'm some sacred cow or something, just because I'm a doctor."

Albert nestles close and asks, "Can I be your sacred bull then?"

She wiggles away from him and sits on the edge of the bed and responds, "Well, you're full of it at least." She stands just out of reach for his long arms to grab her and she retorts, "See, just what your coach said, you're losing a step."

In the kitchen, Big Jim is seated at the table peeling potatoes and Wilma is doing a stack of dishes from the night before. She sees Barbara first and asks, "Did we wake you?"

"No that big lug in my room did. He's pretty upset. I can tell by the way he sleeps, thrashing around." Barbara moves to the sink and pushes Wilma out of the way.

Wilma stops her, "You sit, you're company."

Barbara laughs gently and says, "Two things you need to know about me. First I don't want to be company, I want to help out. And secondly, I can't cook worth a shit, so, I'm going to have to deal with the dishes and let you do some more of your magic."

Resignedly, Wilma moves to the refrigerator and says, "What does Albert like?"

"Put it this way, don't get close to his mouth when he's hungry."

Wilma laughs and points at Big Jim, "I think I understand."

Jim finishes peeling the potatoes and walks into the other room as the phone rings. Sally sitting in the dark crying in the corner catches his attention and he picks up the cordless phone and walks over to sit next to her and gives her a hug. Then he says into the phone, "Big Jim." As he listens, he stands and walks into the kitchen dragging Sally and she perks up when she hears him say, "So he's

OK?" He listens again until he reaches Barbara and says, "Just a second, here's Barbara, explain it to her."

Sally, Wilma and Big Jim look expectantly at Barbara as she listens to the phone. Wilma gently leads Sally away from Big Jim's huge arms and sits her down at the kitchen table kissing her on the forehead.

Albert walks in and stands behind Barbara and they watch as she visibly relaxes and asks a few medical questions and then thanks the person on the phone. Barbara then turns to Jim and Wilma and asks with a serious look. "I've been thinking, once they found out he was in Mississippi, it took them less than 72 hours to send four killers to gun him down, right?"

Albert, deferring to Big Jim as Big Jim responds, "Thereabouts."

Albert nods.

Barbara continues, walking over and kissing Sally, then walking back to the stack of dishes. Reaching in and grabbing the sponge, she uses it to make a point. "Sally sweetie, I'm sorry but they won't stop. We are going to have to hide you and your daddy, or put him somewhere safe."

Big Jim sits down next to Sally and takes her hand as Barbara, washing dishes as she continues, "I have a lot of pull at UCLA Medical Center, but they'll probably guess we would take Uri there. So would it be better to put him somewhere we could control security, or somewhere with little security that they would probably never find?"

Big Jim stands and asks, "Or both. Put him into UCLA with no security under a fake name in the oncology ward but then make a big show of putting him in a security area, or a defensible private facility." He looks at Barbara, "Can we even move him?" Then he looks at the others "I wish Leo was better. He's really good at this type of stuff."

Sally leans over and hugs Big Jim, tears running openly down her cheek.

Chapter 38

Demitre rolls his motorcycle to a stop outside of the small but beautifully appointed home in Venice, California. The neighborhood is filled with expensive homes and nice cars, and he shakes his head in disgust as he removes his helmet and walks to the front door to knock. A surprised but cheerful, short heavy set black man opens the door and checks out the motorcycle leathers that Demitre is wearing and asks, "Demitre?"

Demitre pushes past the man and says, "I don't want to stand around all day, Mr. Jenkins. You left a note saying we were almost ready a week ago. Are they ready or not?"

Jenkins closes the front door and follows Demitre to the living room and answers, cryptically, "These things take time."

Demitre turns and leans threateningly to the smaller man and says, "My boss is starting to doubt you. That is not a good thing, Mr. Jenkins."

"You do want them to work, don't you. Several had to have their wiring harnesses inspected, and there is only one person qualified to inspect them. They're still very hush, hush. You're getting them fresh out of the oven, so to speak."

Demitre walks through the house quickly stepping into the bedroom converted to an office. He steps over to the closed laptop and reaches over touching the side of the laptop for just a few seconds while blocking the view from the door. "Nice house, Mr. Jenkins." Smelling the scent in the room Demitre asks as he walks toward the kitchen, "Speaking of fresh from the oven, are you cooking?"

Jenkins follows him nervously into the kitchen and asks, "What do you want? They'll be done on Friday just like I said."

Demitre opens the oven and closes it saying, "Your bread looks done." Just as his oven timer sounds off. "Banana bread with raisins, Mr Jenkins?"

"No, I don't like raisins."

"A pity. I love raisins. It's a pity to end a friendship just over a lack of raisins." He turns his back on Jenkins and walks out of the kitchen and directly to the front door. "I'll expect raisins on Friday, along with the other items." He opens the door and walks outside.

Ronald Jenkins closes the door and walks back to his kitchen to turn off the oven. He takes the finished banana bread out of the oven and sets it on the granite counter. He puts the pot holders away and walks into his office area and opens his laptop. He enters his password and checks his Cayman Islands account showing that there is $2,120,000.00 left after he paid off his house. Then he sighs and closes his laptop without seeing the shorter-than-normal USB attachment which Demitre had slipped into one of the rear USB ports of his laptop.

Outside, Demitre puts on his helmet and tightens his jacket and stops long enough when his cell phone vibrates to check the screen. He sees his keystroke program has successfully duplicated every keystroke that Mr. Jenkins had just made on his laptop, and says, "Thank you Mr. Jenkins. You won't be needing this after Friday." He turns around and looks directly at the window where Mr. Jenkins is peaking out after him. "Now I will find out how I can get your house too."

He starts his powerful motorcycle and rides slowly away.

Across the street and two houses away, a somewhat out-of-place 1980 Ford van complete with ladder and broken (but duck-taped) side mirror, is parked in the only shady area on the street, under a giant Jacaranda tree. As it appears to be a work van, Demitre disregards it out-of-hand. The van looks empty, but in fact there are two people in the back. One, Evan dialing his phone and the other is Justin watching a light blip blink on and off on a map screen on a piece of electronics wedged between several other sophisticated pieces of equipment. Justin says, "Tell Haywood we've got him."

In Mississippi, Haywood and Margaret are talking about the future and Albert and Big Jim are giving them all the room they can to allow the two to reconcile. As Haywood's cell phone rings, Margaret kisses him and says, "OK, back to the real world. You and I both know this call is important." Haywood answers as she walks toward the kitchen.

"Evan what did you find?"

"A bunch, but best of all we found Demitre. Justin found a guy at Ardberg and we staked his house out and put a GPS on Demitre's freaking Kawasaki Ninja. Nice bike, Cherry would kill me if I got one of those. Did you get Justin's email?"

Haywood looks at his phone and the five unopened emails, "No, sorry, I've been busy."

Chapter 39

The beeping blip on the screen speeds across the map face with amazing agility until it stops somewhere in Santa Monica. Justin calls out the address, which neither he nor Evan recognizes. The van, at a comparative snails pace, finally reaches the location. Pulling up to the Lowes Hotel on Ocean Avenue, there are crowds and limos everywhere and a huge sign reading, "AFM, American Film Market" is hung across the front of the building.

As Justin pulls up to the curb, Evan hops out and strolls toward the door. His movie star good looks cause double takes and whispers, but no one recognizes him. He walks through the first level of security accepting a bag, several magazines and numerous film "one sheets," as he attempts the inconspicuous stroll through the morass of movie wannabes. Prospective starlets and future directors parade the open area of the first floor among the producers, both real and suspiciously unreal. He stands aside as the Troma contingent shows off their latest B movie bombshells dressed and ready for production.

As he approaches the rear of the open and spacious facility, he sees Demitre seated in the bar area with a man wearing a Metro Goldwyn Mayer Badge, and he steps close enough to snap a picture with his smart phone without being detected. As arranged, he walks through the main area and right out the door and down the stairs to the street behind to Justin and the hideous white van.

"He's not staying here. It's a mad house in there. If you'd have dropped me off in a limo, I could have been in someone's next picture."

Justin retorts defending his "invizzo" van, "You're supposed to be invisible. That's what this van does. No one looks at you if you get out of this van."

Justin gets in the back, and Evan takes over driving. He heads down Ocean to where the 10 freeway and the PCH meet. He pulls onto the PCH north toward home. Justin calls from the back, "He's behind us moving fast," and Evan slows down. "Nope, he's not getting on the PCH, he's on Ocean Avenue."

Evan asks, "Where do I get backup there?"

Justin responds, "Not until California street, so turn right and go up the incline. He stopped. Man does he haul ass on that thing."

Evan turns up the incline and Justin yells, "Turn left, he's at the Fairmont Miramar Hotel & Bungalows again."

They park a block from the beach and watch the blip on the screen as it remains stationary. Evan asks, "Should I go in?"

Justin responds, "What if he saw you at the Lowes?"

"No way." Justin stares at Evan, and Evan relents, "OK! You're lonely and don't want me to leave, I get it." Justin shakes his head silently.

Later, Justin starts the van and Evan wakes ups with a start. "We leaving?"

Justin says, "He's either been there for two hours or he's long gone and knows we're following him."

"Did the GPS fall off?"

Justin smiles, "Not unless he took the thing apart. It's made to match the Kawasaki color pattern on his bike." He thinks, "Unless he scanned for bugs. Then it's laying in a ditch and he's on to us."

Justin turns down the California Incline and heads up the coast to Malibu. "Call them and tell them what we learned."

Evan pauses and asks, "So what did we learn?"

"MGM, he has another guy from MGM."

"Why?"

"Well I don't know, but when we do, it might explain why they were dealing with the pervert in the first place. I never understood that connection. What did they need Mr. Kiddy Porn for? Someone that they would need to replace from the same place? Why MGM?"

Evan asks as they drive, "What movie is this from?" as he climbs from the back into the passenger seat, "No Mr.

Bond, I want you to die."

"Goldfinger. They're shooting a "Bond" film somewhere and MGM is traveling with a shitload of cases and carts with all sorts of gear. Perfect! You're a genius!"

Evan looks confused and responds, "We can share the credit. Oh, and stop saying "shitload." You sound like a moron."

"It's from a Mel Brooks film."

"About a moron!"

Chapter 40

Demitre dials his new encrypted cell phone from his hotel room overlooking the beautiful ocean off Santa Monica. As the phone rings, he glances out the window at a beat-up old windowless van and recalls the four men he avoided successfully last year. Why would he think of them? Did they know that FBI agent Haywood? Would he have to deal with them also before he was done? Should he tell Carl about this turn?

"Hello." Carl responds when he sees the phone number on the phone. "Do you have an update for me?"

"The delivery is set. It will be in Egypt on Sunday. I am not pleased with Mr. Jenkins and would deal with him when we are done. He has done things which will draw attention to himself, and I do not feel comfortable, should he be detained and interrogated."

Carl restrains the inner glee he feels being so close to the conclusion of his plan, "A lot can happen in a week. I have sent another team to deal with our other problem. I hope you don't feel slighted. I am otherwise pleased with your service and will consider the bonus earned should the delivery be completed on time."

With the slightest unease, Demitre answers, "Thank

you, sir." Disturbed that he is unable to successfully read his employer, he continues with his premonitions, "There may be an unknown situation, and I am uncertain how they fit into our plan. Last year, when observing the Uri fiasco, four unidentified men became involved and may at least be partly involved in the situation with Mr. Weber."

"Go on."

Demitre measures his words, "They may have assisted Uri, and they may somehow be connected to the FBI agent."

"What could they know?"

"Little. That Mr. Weber did logistics for MGM. If in fact they had something to do with him."

Carl has grasped Demitre's apprehension and asks, "They have no apparent connection. Why do you think they are involved?"

"Because it is my job to consider every possibility. If they are not involved, I will let them alone. It would be creating unnecessary problems. But if they appear and are involved, I will need to dispose of them."

Carl considers and ask, "Why tell me?"

Demitre responds quickly, "Because it is your plan and not mine. They are not the police so they will not act in accordance with established rules of police conduct. If they are involved, I could require additional people to dispose of them. That will cost you money, not me."

"As long as this is not a personal vendetta, and they appear to be interested in our little business deal, you may use the team you have selected. Again, do not get involved yourself."

"Sir, I,..."

"I will not allow you to be at risk." Carl, satisfied that he had gotten his point across, clicks off his cell phone and dials his phone.

In Mississippi, Malcolm's phone rings. hearing Carls salutation he responds with his update, "Sir, we are in place. We have the hospital under surveillance, but have not approached per your instructions."

"I have reason to believe they may move him to LA for his safety. Go ahead and scout to make sure, and do it if the opportunity arises. Don't take any unnecessary risks. If he moves to LA, we will have more men available."

Demitre dials his phone also, "Pavel? Are you in Las Vegas?"

The grizzled leader of the mercenary group responds in accented English, "Yes, operational readiness is at 90%. I have replaced Sergei with a good man, but we have a few nicks that will take a while to heal completely."

"Was there a large black man there when the shooting started?"

"Yes, but he didn't have a gun. There was a small man

and a very large white man doing the shooting, and at least one of them was very good."

Demitre considers his options, "Come to the safe house in Los Angeles and get ready for an assault. I will send a second team for your command, and you should call and see how many more we can call if needed. Plan for a bad scenario. There will be another team sent that will not be under my control. Do you understand what that means?"

Pavel, abandoned by his entire nation when the Berlin wall fell, and abandoned again when things went bad in Chechnya, knew intimately what that meant. "What contingencies will there be?"

Demitre smiled knowing that Pavel was fully aware of the situation. "When the Job is done, I will have an extra Million Dollars U.S. for you to split up any way you want. Be warned, I am being blamed for the situation in Mississippi."

"He is alive? He was hit center mass at least once."

"He is a lucky man, I myself tried to kill him last year. None the less, I am being blamed."

"And we are your right arm."

"Exactly."

Pavel new intimately what his friend and employer meant. "I will have the men ready for anything."

"Thank you, my friend."

Chapter 41

For the first time in years, Justin is truly surprised by something on his computer. He quickly shuts the lid of the laptop and shuts off the sophisticated wi-fi setup. "Whoa!" He opens the laptop backup and runs a full diagnostic on it. Then he runs a diagnostic on his wi-fi and Internet system and then goes into the trap door he set up for the FBI and that's when he finds the truth. There appears to be a new player in the game. A player with technology and bandwidth to change the way the game is played. An enemy? Not the government. Justin pauses to analyze, and then knows. "They're looking for us!"

He stands and then sits, unsure exactly what to do next. Then he stands again and picks up his cell phone and calls Haywood, pacing as if in a cage. "Sorry if I sound scared, .. but I'm scared."

Haywood is sitting with Margaret next to an unconscious Uri. His face gets serious, and he stands and walks to the hall, signaling to Margaret as he leaves. "What's the matter?"

"Remember our jokes about the devil?"

Haywood realizing the question is rhetorical, says, "Yeah."

"Well he's on the Internet. I was doing what I do and then just knew -- dude, I knew I was being looked for."

"What the hell are you talking about? Are you not sleeping or something?"

Justin calms himself, "I run patterns based on what we need. Every time someone checks on something that I don't want them to check without me knowing, I get a signal. It's like being in Lloyd's mine field except I have a tank. I have the best technology, I have the best computer and I have the most bandwidth. So I watch the rest playing, and I'm God. It's my dominion over everyone, until now. I know that someone else has better bandwidth and faster technology. Like I watch others, I can now be detected and manipulated. I'm shut down. We're shut down until I can protect us."

Haywood is startled by the reality. Now his friends are vulnerable. Really vulnerable for the first time. "OK, ok. Were you, uh, discovered? Does he know who you are."

Justin reflects for a moment and answers, "No. I shut down as soon as I was aware which was like only seconds. They know someone exists, but they can't know who it is."

Haywood asks, "If you went back online crunching data like a factory or business, could that throw them off?"

Justin calculates and says, "I Love You man!" and clicks off the phone without saying goodbye.

Haywood walks back into Uri's room and sits next to

Martha, "We need to get back to LA."

Haywood dials Barbara and asks, "Are we set up to move Uri yet?"

Barbara responds, "Maybe an hour or so. But I heard that an employee spotted someone dressed as an orderly, and they ran off when they were confronted. Is that important?"

"It means we're out of time. Are you with Jim and Albert?"

"Yes," and she hands the phone to Big Jim.

Big Jim takes the tiny cell phone and says "Yes?"

Haywood responds, "I'll get two gurneys and a couple of decoys and we'll do a shell game and get Uri out of here now."

Big Jim thinks and says, "I'll go get us a station wagon and we'll decoy an ambulance to the freeway that goes past the airport. That work?"

Haywood, happy to have local help, says, "You bet. Hey, from now on anything done over the computer, we have to consider compromised."

"What about your boy wonder?"

"He's hiding under a rock. Scared and shut down."

Big Jim calculates the ramifications. Then comes a spark of inspiration. He says, "I have a cousin that is a pilot and takes National Guard stuff out to the bases in Nevada all the time."

Haywood smiles, "So you are useful after all." Then says, "I have to go with him you know."

Big Jim smiles, knowing Haywood would go and says, "Maybe I'll make some lame excuse and go too. Maybe send Junior and the kids to Disneyland."

Edgar the Weasel checks his array of monitors and pauses as one particular computer he was scrutinizing through his system comes back online and starts crunching accounting numbers. He says out loud, "So maybe you are an accountant but maybe you are who I am looking for." Realizing he has spent too much time on this one single possibility, Edgar resets his parameters for a universal defensive search and says, "I will go back to work, but I will watch you."

In his man cave, Justin is covered in sweat and has moved several pieces of equipment in an effort to segregate his wi-fi and the other computer units from the one single unit that is currently online and that appears to be crunching accounting figures. Finally, another computer beeps, and he runs to check it. Then he visibly relaxes with a loud, "Woo."

Evelyn looks into the room from the stairs and asks, "You alright, honey?"

Justin cracks a brief smile and responds in his completely exhausted state, "I think so. Sweetie Pie, I think so." Justin stands and walks to the door, kisses her and says, "Now I need to sleep."

Haywood's phone rings, and he sees the number, "Evelyn?"

Evelyn responds, "Yes, Justin is exhausted but wanted me to call and say your idea about setting up like a regular business was brilliant, and he thinks we are safe. Does that make any sense to you?"

Haywood smiles and responds affectionately, "He's a genius, you know."

Evelyn smiles and says, "He's just a fucking Nerd, though. But I love him."

Haywood smiles broadly and says, "Me too."

Chapter 42

On the roof of the hospital, the three armed and serious-looking security people and two nervous-looking orderlies push the gurney out onto the helipad to the waiting chopper. The security people fan out and take position while the orderlies secure the gurney and its occupant to the helicopter and the helicopter rotors start turning with full lift. One of the security people observes a lone man smoking a cigarette on an adjacent rooftop, and the smoking man waves innocently to the armed security man.

After waving and while watching the helicopter lift off the roof, Malcolm taps a button and speaks into the button mike on his collar in his odd South African accent, "Fifty Euro says it's not him."

The static garbled voice on the other end responds, "My money is on the ambulance." Then from the perspective of the man speaking into his button mike, there is an ambulance pulling away from the emergency entrance at the same time. It pulls out to the street and charges off, lights and siren in the direction of the local airport.

Back on the roof, Malcolm responds, "No problem, let them go. Looks like we pack for Los Angeles, just like we were told. "

"Roger that." And the line goes dead.

Malcolm walks to the edge of the building and looking around, takes a deep draw on his cigarette. He almost misses the hearse at the rear end of the hospital building backing up to the entrance clearly labeled "Morgue."

Below doors from the morgue are pushed open. A single man in an orderlies smock pushes a body bag on a gurney rolling it to the back of a hearse. He opens the doors and lowers the gurney to the level of the hearse and starts sliding the top of the gurney into the hearse. Inside the hearse, Haywood pulls the bag fully in and opens the bag as Barbara re-connects the IVs and checks Uri's overall condition. Uri looks up and smiles at Barbara, and she says, "Sorry about this, my friend. I'm afraid that this is as bad as it gets."

Uri smiles and responds, "I will tell you about waking up naked in a dumpster, left for dead. Beating my broken arm against the side trying to find someone to help me. Thank you for caring about me."

On the roof, Malcolm smiles as the hearse drives slowly away from the building. He takes the cigarette from his mouth and tosses it over the side of the building, watching as the ember strikes the asphalt below and bursts into a thousand tiny sparks and dies. He acknowledges the plan and notches his memory bank with the data that he is dealing with smart and dedicated people--people he would like, at least in a different light and a different time.

Barbara continues her observations but is aghast and speechless by what Uri revealed. Haywood offers, "He doesn't talk about that to anyone. He's trying to make you feel appreciated, I think."

Barbara with a tear in her eye asks Haywood, "Then it's true?"

Haywood nods and says, "Yeah, a dumpster, maybe overnight, shot in the head. He's a stronger man than I."

Barbara grabs Uri's hand and holds it tightly all the way to the Army Reserve Base. They head down Military Drive and through the entrance where they are waved through with the highest clearance. Haywood chuckles at the irony, as this onetime, suspected Russian terrorist was now being escorted by a noted surgeon and a retired FBI agent onto a secure military facility where Uri had once killed a man.

As they make the turn approaching the airfield, Haywood has a sudden chill, realizing that he and his friends are moving steadily into the unknown. Against forces they do not understand.

Chapter 43

Enrique Almanzo, who only days ago was called Ernie Alvarez, was seated in a tiny Internet cafe on "H" street in Lompoc, California sipping an excellent dark roast, extra bold cup of coffee. With some trepidation, he was surfing on a brand new email address in a completely random location for just over an hour. All of a sudden, with no logical reason or justification, Ernie shivers the shiver of foreboding. A touch as certain as any paranoid's nightmare, an awareness of the touch of god., at least from a computer standpoint. A touch, that could simply be his imagination, or his worst nightmare. Bereft of the next generation equipment that he had become accustomed to, Ernie, or Ricky, which he still struggled to answer to, knew in his bones that it was time to move again. But where? Complacency had set in already after only one week. He knew what they were and what they would do, but they could *never* find him. Could they?

Ernie stands and waves to the clerk. While deciding if she is a "goth" or just some other out-of-touch teenager attempting to be "hip," he actually considers asking her out. "Is it ok if I leave this computer online for a half hour or so? I'm waiting for something." Ernie drops twenty dollars on the counter for her.

She smiles back and says "Sure. No problem," and Ernie walks past trying to decide if she's only acting like she gives a shit.

On the sidewalk, Ernie shivers again and walks across the street looking around carefully. He decides to test his ridiculous theory. Feeling conflicted and a bit stupid for his paranoia, he decides, against his better judgement, to head across the street to a nearby IHOP for some lunch, with a clear view of the front of the cafe.

Taking his time, hiding behind a menu, he finally orders but keeps the menu as a shield despite the mirrored windows. The ham and eggs are served, but he waits to start until the pancakes arrive. As soon as the hot pancakes are set in front of him, he sets the menu down and puts the excess butter into the his empty creamer containers. He checks his watch and thinks, "Two hours. If they had found me, they would have found me by now." Just as a black suburban drives down the street. The taste of pancakes in his mouth turns to ash as he sees the driver disconnecting a cell phone. The next instant, a missile is fired out the side door out of Ernie's view and goes throw the glass door of the ting Internet cafe. For the briefest second, Ernie guesses the missile is a dud, until less than a heart beat later the entire front of the small shop explodes outward.

The explosion is too small and only rocks the suburban,

but there is no hope for the goth chick and the other unfortunate customers of the tiny shop.

Before the SUV drives away, a passenger armed with an automatic weapon turns the weapon on the brown Toyota Camry parked near the entrance of the shop, which is covered with glass and plaster from the walls of the shop. The car is riddled with bullets, the tires are shredded and the gas tank bursts into flames.

The customers in the IHOP were either lying flat on the floor or were following Ernie out the back door and dispersing in every possible direction. Two blocks away at Ocean Avenue, Ernie grabs his ribs and leans against a building to catch his breath, all the while looking every direction and hoping that the SUV had fled instead of checking to see if he was in dead, or worse, driving around randomly, looking for him.

Ernie knows that his only skill is the computer and now he is struck by the realization that he will never again get to practice what he has always considered his "calling". He knows that if he does he will be "heart attacked" like Forrest by the hit squad he narrowly avoided a couple of days ago or blown to bits and shot full of holes like his poor Camry. Ernie crosses the street to get lost in the park and continues running until he reaches a small bridge that crosses a creek. He slows on the bridge when he sees a small table with an attached bench. He walks to the bench and sits, wiping the sweat from his brow.

Suddenly, as if a light switch is thrown, his few options crystalize in his mind. He could go to the cops and die in a holding cell with his testicles in his mouth. Yes, he had heard with horror the rumors about who he worked for and the price one pays for going to the authorities. The fate of such an unfortunate snitch that was made absolutely certain the very instant that his information was entered into a police database. Ernie's death warrant was already issued, proof was spread across H street.

He could run, a lot of good that would do. He could relearn everything from the ground up and change his well-developed pattern on the Internet and maybe live a few extra weeks.

Or -- and he was surprised that he was seriously considering this one -- he could find the guy that was hunting for him and do him in. Not friggin likely, and even if he killed him, that kind was easy to replace given the right technology. Unless ... then with another bolt of clarity, he knew who had found him. The legendary, Weasel. No one else could, except maybe, ... That guy who found Mr. Weber?

So there were two options left. Become resigned to a life as a greeter at Sam's Club or find that guy that couldn't be found and beg him for help.

One of his less-than-successful assignments at his last job was to discover who had taken the money from the Russian mob and then gave it back. He had been changed to a different job once the funds had been sent back, but his guesses as to who had taken the money were total speculation based in the real world. His best guess was that dude from the cover of Wired Magazine, Justin something or other. Skill off the charts but known as a goofball inventor more than an Über-hacker.

Later, in another small Internet cafe looking up "Wired Magazine" on someone else's account, he finds the right picture. Then, recalling details given during the search, he looks in the Malibu phone directory and finds nothing. OK, to be expected. Then, he assaults the decades-old phone company computer banks and finally finds the number he is hoping for. "Ah."

Chapter 44

Justin is seated in his man cave, but instead of hammering away on his computers, he is staring and contemplating what he can and cannot actually do. Evelyn opens the door to the stairs and says, "Sweetie Pie. Pick up the phone."

He absently turns on the phone he usually ignores hooked to the little-used land line connected to his house and says, "Yes?"

Hesitating, Ernie says, "Hello. You don't know me, but we have something in common."

Justin rechecks the number and says, "Is this a sales call?"

Ready to hang up he hears Ernie say, "No, the thing we have in common is that the same person wants to kill us both. Can I come over?"

"You know where I live?" Justin says overheating.

"We can meet where ever you want, but yes, I know where you live."

At their favorite bar, three of the eight conspirators wait in their corner as an overweight Hispanic man in is early thirties walks through the door. He sees Justin and hesitates as he sees the other two men but walks to the corner. Evan asks, "Want a beer?" and Robert gives Evan a dirty look. Evan retorts, "What?"

Ernie sits and opens, "OK, I need to do some explaining, because you don't know me." The three stare holes through Ernie so he continues. "I work, I mean I worked, for some guys up in Agoura off the freeway and what I was doing was, well, off the books?" He shrugs, "I was like a researcher and a monitor and a bunch of other things. But I knew that what I was doing was crossing a bunch of lines. The job originally was legal until they found I had skills and sort of fired the other three people. They built these really sexy computers, with a ton of built-in security stuff." Justin, Robert and Evan make eye contact, and Ernie makes note. "The place was retrofitted to state-of-the-art, but it was limited by some of the security protocol they used." Ernie hesitates.

Justin says, "Go on."

"You guys aren't cops, right?"

Robert laughs, and Evan says, "We got a guy that works for us, but, no. We are definitely not cops."

"Is he with the FBI?" They look at him but don't answer. "Yeah, I figured. OK, so mostly I just watch and do reviews of stuff. I don't think they trust me really. Last week, I thought they killed you and when I did a full evaluation, I realized that with the amount of gas in that trailer, you should have been vaporized. So you faked it. You knew. Right?"

Justin asks, "So you wanted to talk to us because...?"

"Well, after they were convinced you were dead, or at least some of you, they came after me. I've been running and yesterday I was back online the first time since I took off and the hand of God touched the computer. Someone,..." He can see the recognition in Justin's eyes, "Someone is hunting us. You and me, and we don't stand a chance, I don't stand a chance alone."

"Go to the cops," Evan instructs.

Ernie shakes his head, "And die in some jail cell with my testicles in my mouth? I don't think so."

Justin looks at the other two and asks them off-handedly, "He could work for me?"

"Do you trust him?" They ask simultaneously.

Chapter 45

The sexy Ninja motorcycle pulls to a stop at the greasy spoon near the intersection of Lincoln and Venice Boulevard in Venice and picks up an order of food that has been called in by Edgar. Demitre does not consider himself a gofer or a lackey, but they both appreciate the greasy burgers and french fries from the tiny diner and this is the best way to make sure his computer eyes and ears take nourishment. Even though that nourishment is a greasy burger.

Back on his bike and driving the few blocks away, Demitre pulls over in front of Edgar's computer lair and carries the plastic bag of lunch to the front door. Pulling out the key, he enters the untouched, unused living area and walks through to the office where Edgar has burrowed his discarded food containers and several discarded pieces of clothing leaving himself barely a path to make it to the bathroom. Edgar looks over his shoulder and asks, "Burgers?"

Demitre holds up the familiar plastic bag and smiles. He sets the food down within reach of the bizarre man and swats a few flies that have also discovered the waste in the room. Edgar turns and nods in thanks and says, "I almost had them both. The one we are looking for and the one that worked for you."

Demitre responds, "The one that worked for me is no longer a problem."

Edgar says, "I think the other one was somehow using the computer of a Malibu accounting firm. So, the one in Lompoc is not a threat anymore."

Demitre adds "Yes. The other will be done when ever you find him."

Again Edgar nods and responds, "It's just a matter of time."

Justin hears a beep from a computer not hooked up to the Internet and turns to see that Demitre's motorcycle has stopped at an address for 15 minutes, so he jots down the address and texts it to Roberts to review in his new Realtor software. Ernie is completely in awe of the setup that Justin has assembled. "This is smoking hot! This is better than what they have."

"Except they have bandwidth and processing power that I simply can't comprehend. It was like the touch of god."

"Exactly. But your stuff, do you link the systems? Wait, can it just be the bandwidth?"

"I don't know. Maybe?"

Justin's phone rings and he checks the number puts it on speaker and says, "Hi Robert. You're on speaker. What did you find?"

"Nice house on the market after a seizure by the feds for something. One of the notes says that the previous owner, installed a pair of CRS-3 routers, does that mean anything?"

Both Ernie and Justin's mouths drop open. Justin says, "State of the friggin art."

Ernie says, "Supposedly scalable to a total capacity of up to 322Tbps. Faster than,... Faster than..."

Justin interrupts, "God."

Robert completely lost asks, "Is this good?"

Demitre and Edgar are munching on their burgers, Edgar takes a bite of his burger and wipes the grease from his chin. "I keep going back to who *could* take the Russians money and the answer itself eliminates almost everyone. Nobody should have been able to find it unless it was a complete accident and they were looking for something completely unrelated. So they have an incredible amount of processing power and they simply stumbled over it. They would have to look at the three men that accessed it and know about them before Alexandre died. Then, they would have to sneak past the security system I put together and all without leaving a trail. I ask who on earth, could do this and I get no answer, none. So I ask who and remove one item of data from the facts, and after a couple of tries they give me a burnout, living in Malibu. He has done nothing for at least 2 years since he sold his company. He's married and he does nothing. I tried to attack his computer and it's off line. He's crawled into a hole."

"Get me his name and address anyway when you find it."

Chapter 46

The tarmac at March Air Reserve base was a comfort and relief after the turbulence of the military flight, but totally untraceable as the old-school Humvee driven by Evan rolls out of the base and up the 215 Freeway towards Malibu. The call had been made to the UCLA Medical Center, oncology, with 24-hour care supervised by a retired doctor friend Barbara and Albert. Close enough for a visit, with enough room for the comforts of Sally, close and yet not in the way. The main concern for everyone about Sally was that there were no friends around her age.

The mind-set of the now ten conspirators was that the ordeal would be over in a few days at most. As they all sit in Evan's house, Margaret included, Justin and Evan lay out their discovery. Justin observes, "MGM appeared totally incidental with Lloyd but was cemented when Demitre set up the arrangement with the logistics man from the MGM. A tenuous connection at best, but the common link none-the-less. Their educated guess was that although the shooting of the preliminary footage of the next "James Bond" film in Turkey was months away, the first shipment of equipment and props to Istanbul was scheduled for Friday. Three days away."

Haywood asks, "Props?" Like...?"

Evan offers, "Like missiles and rocket launchers."

Robert adds, "And they have to look exactly real."

Justin offers "And maybe we found the guy causing us so much problems with the computers. But we don't have any idea what to do with him. We have a suggestion, though, if you want to hear it."

Haywood is impressed, "A solution?"

Justin corrects, "A suggestion." He talks into his cell phone, "Ernie come on in."

The door at the top of the stairs opens, and Ernie walks down the stairs apologetically, "Uh, hi everyone." The room is not used to unknown people but they are cordial because he is invited. He starts right in, "OK, I need to be out front with you, I'm in this to save my own neck. I was the Internet eyes for the bad guys right up to the point in time that they tried to kill me." He has their attention. "Following orders, I pushed the button that blew up the computer that Lloyd had. I found Forrester for them and, well, I know what they do. But I didn't do anything to anyone. My job was mostly legal, but I know better, I was a bad guy. OK."

Barbara is pissed because she knows he was indirectly responsible for what they are in the middle of. But she listens as he continues, "They have the most awesome computing setup ever put together, and because of that we are all at risk. Especially Justin and me. When we're online we leave a scent because of the way we operate. Just like a fingerprint and that print is traceable. So we have an opportunity to use their advantage against them. By old-fashioned leg work, you found out where the Weasel is. He's the guy that designed the computers, he's the guy that protects the mob's money and he's the one that we need to eliminate. I say that, and I kind of mean it. Most hackers you can replace with the next nerd in line. Then there's guys like Justin and the Weasel. They *are* the Internet."

Albert reasons, "You have yet to tell us your "suggestion" as to how we can take the Internet back."

Ernie continues, "Look I know how you guys feel about this, so I'm not going to say kill him, which you definitely should do. Since we won't, we could corrupt his information. One problem with super fast stuff is that the human is now the slow part."

Justin inserts, "I had a peek into their gear. But not enough. So Ernie had this idea..." He then signals to Ernie to continue.

"So we write a virus that looks like mamma. No one says no to mamma. The units speak to each other and they use a code, and pretty much anything that comes in with that code is allowed. The beast is so fast that even if the Weasel finds it, he'll never be able to close it down." The problem is I don't know how to get past the CRS-3 routers."

Justin adds, "Not to be a cold blanket, but we have three

days to find out how to do that and simultaneously shut down what we think is a an international weapons-smuggling ring."

Haywood offers, "But we know where the weapons are going. But not actually what they are. So we could be looking at genuine props for the movie or the actual weapons."

Robert asks, "I thought you were set on those new shoulder fire missile thingies?"

Barbara nods in recognition of the dilemma, "But we don't really know do we?"

Haywood shrugs, "Nope."

Chapter 47

Big Jim takes the mail out of the mailbox and starts backup the driveway. He walks up on the porch past the newly filled bullet holes along the exterior wall to the house without noticing them. Instead, he is staring at a parcel that appears to be holding a disk of some sort. He opens it and pulls out a DVD. He steps into his study and slides the disk into the player. With his eyes fixed on the machine, he sits down, grabs the remote and presses play. A presentation starts. The lettering that comes on the screen reads, "To be forwarded to Media and Police forces only." As the images start, a man in a white smock, looking very scientific, standing in front of a tiny winged missile, points at the missile and says,

"The Ardberg 9IIA's Phase II tri-mode seeker can peer through storm clouds or battlefield dust and debris to engage fixed or moving targets, giving the warfighter a capability that's unaffected by conditions on the ground or in the air. Ardberg Phase II is a new 11.5-pound, 21-inch long, precision-guided gravity-dropped bomb specifically designed for employment from manned and unmanned aircraft systems. Phase II is more than two inches shorter than the Phase I design and has foldable fins and wings, enabling employment from the U.S. military's common launchers. Phase II's easier assembly will make the system simpler to manufacture on a large scale."

"The key points: At less than 12 pounds and 21 inches, 911A is the smallest air-launched weapon in the Ardberg portfolio, with built-in digital semi-active Laser sensors on a single gimbal. The result is a powerful, integrated seeker that seamlessly shares targeting information between all three modes, enabling them to engage fixed, relocatable or moving targets at any time of day and in adverse weather conditions. Small enough to be employed from the common two-man, shoulder-operated launch tube. Either shoot and forget, or shoot and decide before it gets to where it's going."

On the screen the missile is aimed at a drone and fired, then in mid air it changes directions and hurtles at a target tank and explodes with devastating results. The impact is startling for such a tiny payload. The second missile is fired, and the men flee into a bunker as the missile streaks into the sky and knocks down a target drone zipping across the sky. The voice starts again. "With uses against sub-sonic and super sonic aircraft."

Big Jim dials his cell phone and calls Haywood. "Good morning. I just chills Haywood. I saw what would be on my shopping list if I was a terrorist."

Haywood yawns and looks at the clock and responds,

"You think this is what we're looking for then?"

"Haywood, this is every terrorists wet dream. Self correcting, shoulder launch, my god! This has almost no value to a conventional army unless they're battling another conventional army. This is truly scary shit."

Haywood kisses Margaret and gets out of bed. "Can you send it to me?"

At Evan's house the rest gather, including Ernie who now has a few friends in the group and Haywood presses the button on the remote to start the DVD. At the end of the presentation, Haywood speaks, "To be clear, I have no idea if this is what they are shipping, but it's brand new and the first order ships in two weeks. Also, this is the unity we considered last week but had no information."

Barbara starts, "But we are expecting this..."

Haywood interrupts, "Friday, yes I know, but this is where we are if something else doesn't come up. I'll call McHugh and try to get the FBI fired up, but I can't make any promises until I get cleared on that drug thing."

Albert asks, "Are you going to tell them about the Frenchman and the Senator?"

Haywood pauses before answering, "Not unless it comes up. It sounds too much like sour grapes. I want to stay on point. What we know."

Barbara adds, "But we aren't sure about the missiles

even."

Haywood shakes his head, "They have to believe me."

Robert suggests, "I have an idea. We can call that Homeland Security guy Trimble and tell him we're sure this is the target and the day is Friday. If we're right, it should freak the bad guys out completely. Maybe cancel the plan altogether."

Albert nods and continues the thought, "At least we can delay them, maybe convince them it's too dangerous."

Haywood counters, "They already are looking for us, right Justin?"

Justin and Ernie both nod and Justin says, "This Weasel guy is going to find us. It's just a matter of time. We can't be patient."

Ernie adds, "I know I don't have a vote, but you cannot let the Weasel live. He will not let you live. The guy he works for isn't Demitre. The guy he works for is the Devil. You need to put as much space between you and the Devil as possible. I am a dead man if he lives, and I'm sure Justin is a bigger target than me."

Haywood asks, "So we could blow up his house instead of the virus."

Barbara starts to protest, "NO! To many innocents. If we are actually thinking about taking him out to save Justin and Ernie, then it has to be after the shipment is stopped and one on one."

Justin responds, "Thanks, but right now we can't get back online to find out any of the logistics yet."

Ernie raises one finger and says, "Justin, I have a thought on that after we get done here."

Haywood raises his hand, "Ernie, that may be the single biggest thing stopping us, so go ahead."

Ernie, reticent at first, shrugs and starts, "They want me, OK. But they *really* want Justin. I mean I heard about how pissed he was when Justin hacked that mob money. That was his defenses Justin lit up and left untraceable. Pissed, OK? So what if we give him something he really wants? Justin."

Everyone in the room takes exception, but Justin stills them, "Wait, let's here what he has to say."

The group settles down, and Ernie, a bit sheepishly, continues, "When I blew up the other computer, I had really mixed feelings about it. So I ran a diagnostics on the program, and it seems that all of them have that same "defensive security setup'. Even the ones that Edgar uses, because they don't want it messed with or found out."

Justin stands up, "So maybe I go online and he starts chasing me, and you can sneak in the back door and blow up his computer?"

Ernie continues, "Not really. Maybe I act like you, and you sneak in. The problems though, are many. First, we can't try until someone is on the hook. Second we aren't sure we can do it and last, if we fail, you are all neck deep in trouble."

Justin considers the options and offers, "We're in it already. We let him go and we're found out, eventually." He looks at Ernie and Ernie nods knowingly. "So...?"

Barbara says adamantly, "No killing!"

Ernie hides his disappointment but says, "OK. I get it."

Chapter 48

Ave Verum Corpus is rarely heard with lyrics and as such is rarely considered anything but a masterpiece of simplicity and wonder that Mozart often was uniquely capable of. That it was in actuality an Easter song referring to the death of Christ, "Hail, True Body" never crosses Carl's mind as he sits in front of his fireplace, eyes closed, and conducts the exquisite piece with his finger in the air, uninterrupted by the occasional pop from the fireplace. The sound from the impressive one-of-a-kind stereo system allows every harmonic and every nuance to be heard as if it is being played into the room.

The moment is perfect, until Carl's cell phone rings and breaks the spell. "Merd!" He presses the remote before he picks up his cell phone. Looking at the number, his anticipation takes over, "Is it ready?"

Demitre responds, "I believe so. Your men from Mississippi are here, the leader, Malcolm, has some interesting ideas on how to root out our pests. I do like him. They have gone to ground because of Edgar's persistence and flair for the truly unique computer setup we assembled. Yes, if all goes as planned, they should be out of the country Friday."

Carl relaxes, "Excellent. Then I assume you will take care of the pests?"

"As well as a few others."

"Could any of them be useful in the future?"

Demitre frowns but knows it is not his boss's weakness that makes him ask, "The risk is too high, and it has been so easy to replace pawns as needed."

Carl sighs as if he truly cares and says, "C'est la guerre. May I go back to Mozart now?"

Demitre smiles and responds, "If you mix in a touch of Beethoven now and then."

Carl leans back and restarts the music with the remote, closes his eyes and is transported into Clarinet Concerto in A. After almost falling into Mozart's trance, Carl shifts, presses the stop on the remote and dials another number.

On the other end, Malcolm answers, "Yes, Boss."

"Tell me everything."

"Demitre does not tell me everything, but the shipment is due Friday, so we can get it to the studio for shipment Friday night for loading on Saturday morning. Then it will be in Turkey Sunday. He has a crew of 8 mercenaries to protect the plan. It looks good. I think he has done a good job. But like I said, Demitre has not told me all the details."

Carl understands, "He is hurt because you are my man. He is a good man, but you are my eyes. If he succeeds, you will go home with full pockets. If he fails, ... shoot him.

His men are yours to deal with."

Chapter 49

Haywood, Robert, Evan, Albert and Justin sip beers at the sports bar. Haywood sneaks a peek around the room and ask, "Do you trust Ernie?

Puzzled by the question, Justin responds, "Do I trust him like I trust you, no way. But he's afraid for his life and we seem to be the best solution, so..." He trails off.

Haywood takes a sip of beer and says, "Yeah, me too. Is he useful?"

"He has stuff on their proprietary gear that I am positive they didn't know he had. He's good but he knows his limitations, which is a good combination. I'm like way better, but sometimes I get ahead of myself. He is a lot of help. That much I know."

Haywood asks, "So tell me why you think this "pinch" thing will work. Ernie doesn't seem so sure."

Justin takes a deep draft of the designer pale ale and sighs, "Techno speak 101, OK?"

"I'll try to keep up. Robert, Evan, you both listen and keep your remarks to yourself."

Robert says, "What about Albert?"

Haywood offers, "He doesn't interrupt stuff; he tries to hear and decide. Besides, he pays me, so I'm going to kiss his ass."

Albert says, "Damn right!"

"OK?" Justin unfolds a napkin and takes out an ink pen, "Technically it's not a pinch but a NNEMP, or Non Nuclear electromagnetic pulse. They're not new technology, they just aren't built by civilians. The theory is a low inductance capacitor discharged into a single loop antenna or a microwave generator into what would be called an explosively pumped flux compression generator." He can sense the eyes glazing over, but continues, "The trick is to achieve the frequency characteristics of the pulse needed for coupling to the target. I designed wave shape circuits and the biggest vacuum tube I could find that was suitable for microwave conversion. So far so good?"

Haywood responds , "I'm ok up to NNEMP." Justin laughs.

Albert says, "Justin, just hearing your confidence makes me happy. Can you dig that?"

Justin smiles and nods affectionately and says, "Our dilemma is the range. It's all based on theoretical computations because I've never set one off before. It could be too small or it could blow up the block." Sensing Haywood's concerned look, he adds, "I mean short circuit the whole block's TVs or toaster ovens, cell phones, stuff like that."

Haywood reflects, "Collateral damage?"

Justin smiles and says, "Better than the other kind, I suppose."

Haywood asks a consensus of the group, "So do you understand, and what do you think about Ernie's new plan?"

Justin nods, "It's solid. The pinch knocks out his computer, turns it into rubbish. He always has a backup. If we can get him outside for one minute, Evan can get in and plant the USB adapter. Even if he starts the boot of the backup immediately, we should be able to get it in before it's finished and I'm in. I set the hook, and we can read their mind. More importantly, we're back on line. It's a scary thing this close to their delivery. Everything may have already changed, and we can't find out until we're back on line."

Evan asks, "The last one blew up. What's to keep this one from blowing up?"

Justin offers, "Well the Weasel designed the system from what Ernie says. So he's not going to blow himself up."

Haywood continues, "So if he comes out the door, Ernie tells Evan to go in. If he doesn't come out, Ernie goes to the door, in the meter-reader outfit and asks if his power is out. I get that. If it goes bad, then they have the pinch in the tool box. Isn't that bad?"

Justing smiles, "Honestly, I doubt that it would ever lead to me. But it's homemade so worst case I might have to make up a lie and hire Gerry Spence to keep me out of jail.

I'll live. But the plan is we grab it before we go."

Haywood decides, "If it goes the way Ernie thinks, we grab it and bail out and we own them. So, we're all okay with it?"

Albert says, "Unless the cops show up too early. But I guess the risk of that is pretty small."

They all nod supporting the plan and sip their beers.

Chapter 50

Near the beach in Venice, the beat-up white van is parked under the shady branches of an old oak tree, a mere two houses down from where Edgar is entrenched. In the back of the van, Ernie, with a shaved head, bushy black eyebrows and Harry Potter glasses, is dressed like a meter reader from the electric company. He is working with a small USB plug while wearing a head set with microphone. Ernie asks over the headset, "Justin, dude, what if he has a battery backup?"

Justin cracks back over the head set. "He has a battery backup! Do you have a battery backup?"

Ernie says meekly, "Yeah, but that doesn't ..."

Justin breathes and says, "If he has a battery backup, it will be fried just like his computer, and he will have to completely reboot his backup computer when the power comes back on and when will that be?"

Ernie answers, "Sorry. OK I get it."

Justin is at his workbench at home assembling a tiny gizmo as he checks his monitors casually.

"What if he doesn't come out of the house?"

Evan shakes his head from the front seat and yells, not remembering he is wearing a headset, "Ernie, you're a weenie!" and then immediately, "Sorry guys. I know, the headset." He puts his hand over the mike on the headset and says, "You are like the worst chicken for a bad guy."

Robert hears on his headset and snickers, "Relax, you'll knock on the door and he'll come to the door."

"What if he knows my face?"

Haywood can't stay out of it any longer, "Have you ever met him?" Before he can answer he asks, "Have any of them taken a picture of your face?"

Ernie finally relaxes, "OK, OK. I get it."

Albert inserts, "The odd thing is that Robert isn't whining about anything."

Robert, incensed says, "Me? Your talking about me!"

Haywood, Evan and Justin laugh until Robert gets the joke, "Assholes. Ernie, you will be so happy when this is behind us. They only pick on you because you're an idiot, though."

Ernie laughs nervously and picks up the gear and asks, "OK so are you sure about the range on that thing?"

Justin stops working and says, "No, but somewhere between 40 and 60 feet. Leave your phone off, remember to turn off all the head pieces right before we pop it. Then just turn "em back on."

Robert, trying to be an asshole, asks, "You don't have a pacemaker do you, Ernie?"

Ernie makes a face and says, "Screw you guys. I'm not

buying the first round now."

Albert laughs and Evan says, "No more Mr. Moneybags."

Justin asks, "Ernie, you got the USB thing or did you give it to Evan?"

Ernie pushes the tiny device into a lead-lined box and hands it to Evan and says, "I just handed it off, OK?"

Justin says, "OK, flip on the infrared then."

Ernie flips on the infrared device and points it at the house and responds, "It's lit up, and it looks like there are two guys in the house. Oops, wrong house. OK, right house now."

Albert, Robert and Evan are laughing, and Haywood says sternly, "Guys!" They instantly snap into action mode. "Jesus, you guys are like my grandkids."

Ernie says, "One person in the office, the room with the blacked-out windows." He shuts down the unit and says, ..."and, the infrared is off."

Haywood instructs, "Evan get into position. You have the gizmo and the key?"

Evan says, "Yep'er."

Robert mocks him over the head-set, "Yep'er."

Evan shakes his head and refuses to be sucked in, "I'm moving."

Robert says, "Me too," and he steps out of a different van, this one green with "ABE'S PLUMBING" scrolled on the side. Robert has a dirty tee shirt and pants showing his butt crack, and he is lugging an enormous tool box toward the front   of Edgar's house. Robert asks, "Where is Demitre?"

Justin checks and says, "Still at Paramount on Gower."

Evan asks as he approaches the neighbors fence, "Why not at MGM?"

Haywood responds, "We'll worry about that latter. Guys, let's do this."

Chapter 51

Like a crack team, Robert sets the tool box in the bushes directly in line with the office where Edgar is set up and walks to the front door, but then changes his mind and walks back to the green van.

Evan asks, "Is this lead going to protect this thing?"

Justin responds seriously, "Yes, just don't hold it close to your testicles."

Evan stops in his tracks and Ernie, Albert, Haywood and Justin all laugh. Haywood adjusts his demeanor and says, "Guys, OK?"

Evan stops, surrounded by the weeds and garbage of the next door neighbors yard, perches on a box holding a small ladder previously stashed in the yard, and says, "I'm in position, you miserable bastards," and everyone snickers again but stops immediately.

Justin says, "Ready Haywood."

Haywood, ready, says, "All electronics shut down. A three count in your head, and then it goes. Right?" Everyone says check, so Haywood responds, From Now!" He flips off his gear and continues counting in his head, "Three, two, one, ZERO!"

The faces of all look apprehensive, yet apparently,

nothing at all happens.

Then, slowly, the neighbors on both sides of the street come out of their front doors mulling around. Ernie turns back on his headset. "Testing Testing. Dude, if it worked, it fried everyone for like a whole block!"

Haywood is startled and says, "Too many people."

Then the front door of the target house opens, and Edgar walks out. Seeing the other people, he walks toward the neighbor with the crappy backyard where Evan is waiting and Ernie says, "Go Evan, he's out front."

Haywood yells, "Ernie, stay in the van!"

As Edgar walks to the neighbor and asks what happened, Evan has already gotten to the back door and found it unlocked. He slips into the kitchen area and through to the office. He spots the fried unit and sees the backup starting to boot on a separate battery pack and slips the tiny USB into a rear USB port, flips a tiny switch, puts the computer back to what he believes is exactly where it was and slips back into the kitchen. At the fence he asks, "Where is he?"

Ernie says, "He's going back in the house, are you done?"

Evan climbs the small ladder and pulls it over the fence behind him and steps in something mushy and says, "Crap!"

Albert ask, worried, "What happened?"

Evan repeats, "Crap! I stepped in crap! OK?"

Ernie giggles and says, "The neighbors are back in their houses too. All clear."

Evan hurdles the fence and walks slowly to the front of the house looking around and seeing all of the neighbors have gone back into their houses. Seeing no neighbors, he picks up the large tool box and heads the van. Evan starts the well-tuned engine, puts the van in gear and drives away casually.

Justin asks, "Are we all clear?"

Ernie says, "Evan and I are out, and Robert is already gone. Although you guys act like a squad of baboons, I must say that was pretty ..." He never gets the words out as an explosion rips through Edgar's house knocking out all of the windows and knocking the front door off its hinges.

Haywood asks, "Justin, what happened?"

Justin reflects, "Well, I think Ernie just killed Edgar."

Ernie shouts in the back of the van, "Wait a minute, wait a minute!"

Evan stops the van and Ernie runs out of the side door directly to Edgar's door. By this time the neighbors are back out watching. As it's clear he intends to go inside, one neighbor yells, "Don't go in, the whole thing might blow." Ignoring him, Ernie runs in and fights his way through debris to the office where Edgar's mutilated body is shoved against the side wall. Both computers exploded. Ernie grabs the USB unit and slides it into his pocket, then makes his way out the door. Outside he shakes his head "no" to the neighbors and walks back to the van and gets in.

Ernie tells Evan, "Go!"

Haywood asks concerned, "Ernie, why go back inside?"

"I had to make sure he was dead. Oh, I got the USB thing, let's call it payment."

Haywood, fuming, yells into his mike, "Payment? Evan, drive slow until you're around the corner. Then we need to talk."

By the time they are around the corner, Ernie has stripped off his uniform and slipped on a Dodgers cap and sunglasses and is wearing jogging shorts and a tee. He then says, "Sorry guys, He had to die. I'm out now, so I'm leaving." He opens the side door, and Evan, seeing the door open, stops the van. Ernie hops off while it's still moving and he jogs off. In their headsets they hear him say, "Now I can call Demitre and tell him it was my doing, or you can try to catch me and have them come after you. You decide."

In the background they hear several sirens, and Haywood instructs, "Evan's house. Now! Call the ladies. Now silence on the line."

Chapter 52

Ernie rounds at the corner, already winded from the short run, and stops to peek back at the van from a safe distance. He feels touch of remorse in his heart for not telling them that the security system would go into self-destruct mode when the pinch went off. Ernie knew that his only means of survival from the Frenchman, would be that the Weasel and his "stuff" be vaporized. Maybe he was a bad man after all. Selecting a random direction, Ernie walks off as he considers dialing his phone, now, thanks to Justin, set up in full stealth mode. Imagine being able to bounce off three cell towers despite the range and confuse anyone's search. Justin was a genius. Way out of his league. But sometimes the will for survival had a measurable value.

Nearly $9,000.00 in his pocket, a couple of tricked-out toys he stole from Justin and the rest of the world to hide in and he would just have to be OK with that. The tiny USB toy itself was worth the trouble. But he did have a debt to pay to Justin and the others, so he dialed the phone.

Seated back on his motorcycle outside of "Pinks" around the corner from the Paramount studios, Demitre, as yet still unaware of the recent disaster, sees the somehow familiar phone number on his screen and answers the phone, "Hello?"

Ernie, as cheerfully as possible says, "Pop goes the weasel, Demitre. You tried to kill me twice, and now I'm free. I won't come after you unless you try again. But your weasel is gone, so I'm safe. Unless you insist on doing something stupid."

Demitre is stunned at the absurdity of the jest. His English falters for just a second until he regroups and asks, "What are you talking about?"

Ernie lies, "I also popped his security system and exploded his computer. I think I may have damaged a couple of TVs in the neighborhood though too. Venice is such a quiet neighborhood, until all of those fire trucks showed up with the lights and sirens."

Demitre, now in full-blown panic mode, realizing that if this is true he has lost the upper hand, "You did this? You?"

"Yes, me!"

At Evan's house, the ten reevaluate the plan. Haywood, still reeling from the deception, offers, "We are busted. We went from having an edge to being known to the enemy."

Justin responds, "Not necessarily. Do you recall your history of World War II?"

Haywood assumes a look on his face that is a cross between annoyed and interested by the question, he challenges Justin, "OK?"

Justin continues, "The Germans were the boss of all of Europe as long as they had air superiority. As soon as enough of their planes had been shot down and the Americans were fully in the fight, they took over the air superiority and the tide turned."

Haywood quibbles, "Not exactly that simple, but I get your point. You think that us, you, controlling the Internet and air waves gives us the edge."

Justin responds, "We own their logistics again. We just have to figure out which box and where and we can do this."

Haywood stands and looks specifically at the ladies and says, "At the cost of our wives and families. This means that they will probably know who we are and where to find us. I'll give you ten to one odds that Ernie is now working for Demitre."

Albert responds, "That's absurd. He's scared to death of those guys." Evan and Robert join him.

Haywood retorts, "You ever hear the expression, "Making his bones'?"

They nod yes, and Haywood continues, "Ernie has made his bones. He's proven he is not to be threatened or messed with, and he's even killed someone." They consider the possibilities and Haywood continues, "Demitre knows he has lost his "air superiority", and he needs to do something to help shift the balance back. Now he has a guy he thinks just beat his best man. He's probably scared shitless of the French guy, right? He can offer him the Weasel's cut, he's not out a single penny from his own pocket." Haywood looks at Justin, "Now "dude', you need to find out if Ernie stole any of your gizmos.

The look of shock hits Justin's face first. "We can't track his cell phone. But we can listen in if he uses it."

After a seconds stunned silence, Haywood asks, "Really?" Justin shrugs, deep in thought. Haywood asks, "Can you set it up to ring to my phone when he does something?"

Justin thinks and says, "It won't ring when he calls out, it'll just show up on the dial. But you'll get a special ring when he gets a call. Gimme me your phone."

Haywood asks, "When will I get it back?"

Justin responds, "As soon as I enter a ten-digit code-number. You're starting to sound like Robert."

Robert, deep in thought snaps back and retorts , "Me?"

Ignoring the banter, Albert stands and says, "Then the women need to leave the area until this is over."

Barbara grabs her husbands arm and retorts, "I was gone a week, and there is no way ..."

Albert interrupts and looks into her eyes, "We won't be able to do this if you guys are in danger, and you will be, either way. Sweetie, please."

Barbara sits back in a huff with her arms crossed.

Haywood looks at Margaret and asks her, "I need you to be safe. I can't do this if I think you may be in any danger."

Haywood and Margaret hug,

Barbara responds, "I'm not going anywhere. I have to take care of Uri. So If you girls want to go, that's up to you. End of conversation."

Chapter 53

Demitre is seated on his motorcycle on the end of Edgar's street in Venice watching the police and fire department come and go from the house that used to be Edgar's. Eventually a gurney is wheeled from the home across the uneven debris field that was a front yard and walkway.

He presses the redial button for the number on his screen and listens as Ernie's voice says, "Demitre?"

Demitre fights back the bile growing in his throat and says, "You have proved yourself to me. Will you work for me?"

"You tried to kill me twice, why should I work for you?"

"Stupid boy, for the money. What do you think? You knew who we were. We assumed you were a liability. Now we know you are not. This is business. I am looking for a man with certain skills, which you possess. There has been a recent ... vacancy left to fill."

Ernie asks, "What benefits do you offer?"

Demitre smiles knowing he has found his replacement, "No stock options, if that's what you mean. You will receive Edgar's full cut, which should be over $400,000.00. We get the missiles out of the country, then you can disappear if you want to. Unless you like to work."

The silence makes Demitre smile, "You work for me, not him. That means you are out of his field of control. Do you know what that means?"

Ernie's silence is finally broken as he asks, "I have conditions, do you want to hear them?"

"Certainly."

Ernie gets serious, "I work from a remote location, and if you or your little army shows up, I come after you for keeps. I killed Edgar, I can get to you."

Demitre smiles, "You don't trust me. I understand that I have not earned your trust. You understand that was only business. Now you work for me. Do you need a computer?"

"Not one of yours."

Haywood presses a button on his Blackberry and touches the rewind button and presses the play button, and he hears Ernie's voice say, "Not one of yours."

He follows the explicit instructions given to him by Justin and copies the file and then converts the audio to an "e-mail-able" file. He sends the file to an email address and then dials his phone.

The phone is answered with, "Agent McHugh."

Haywood says, "Boss, I just sent you a file. Please listen to it and call me. I have some stuff you need to hear."

"You know this is under Homeland Security."

Not when you hear what I need to tell you."

Chapter 54

In his large corner office, McHugh has three men in the room to hear the recording. One of the men familiar with audio alterations and editing, while the other two experts in terrorism.

McHugh says, reading the instructions from the file, "OK here it is. Demitre Velicoff and Ernie Alvarez, Alvarez starts."

He presses the play button and they listen as Ernie's voice says, "Demitre?"

"You have proved yourself to me. Will you work for me?"

"You tried to kill me twice, why should I work for you?"

"Stupid boy... " the four men listened intently to the recording. "We get the missiles out of the country, then you can disappear if you want to. Unless you like to work." Durning the moment of silence following this comment, the four men look at each other. They listen to the rest of the conversation, and then McHugh looks at the others and says, "Don't ask where it came from. I'm going to call him right now. Comments."

One asks McHugh, "If this is real, then it should be Homeland Security?"

McHugh says, "Let's hear him out."

"Who is it?"

McHugh blanches for a second and says, "Samuel Haywood."

The three men roll their eyes but remain quiet, respecting McHugh. One finally blurts, "This guy is on an express train to the loony bin."

"I said we'd listen. OK?" They nod.

McHugh dials. Knowing he has a limited leash, Haywood starts right up when he answers the phone, "Let me start with two things, and Hello, whomever you have on the line. I have reason to believe that Mr. Trimble, of Homeland Security has been paid off on this. I have proof that he has received money from a source out of the country and that he called a man in the south of France immediately following my visit. That man called a senator's residence in Washington DC that day, and I was busted on the bogus drug charge the next morning. Mysteriously, a half hour before the media was notified by the Tacoma police, the good senator called the FBI to have my retirement challenged. No way on earth he could have known about that when he called unless someone told him it was going to happen."

The man on McHugh's left interrupts, "Why are you arguing your innocence to us Mr. Haywood?"

"A man at Ardberg paid off his house with almost $200,000.00 and has just over of two million dollars in a

Cayman Islands account. The same Swiss account that put the money in that account bought a Gulfstream that hauled hit men to Mississippi where they shot a deputy sheriff." The line is silent and Haywood senses that he is too close to this and it all sounds like a conspiracy theory based on sour grapes. "Look, I don't care about me. I'll be fine. What I'm saying is that I believe based on evidence that you cannot use in court that Homeland Security has been compromised for the express purpose of shipping a crate of next-generation shoulder launch-missiles. Missiles with technology capable of shooting down Air-force One as example. With the intent that they be sold to people that will not hesitate to kill Americans."

Sensing disaster, McHugh says to Haywood, "OK, We've got it, I'll call you back."

The same man to the left of McHugh stands and walks to the door. Looking back he offers, "If you think I'm going to accuse a sitting senator and frontrunner for the next presidency of participating in international terrorism, you're out of your fucking mind." He turns to leave and then turns back, "This coming from a guy who's facing a hearing because a bunch of serious drugs was found in his house. This is desperate." He looks at McHugh, "You have to be kidding me, right?"

As the other two men file out of the room, McHugh dials Haywood's number and waits. Haywood answers,

"Haywood."

McHugh says, "You just got shot down. Send me what you have. I'll see if we can salvage anything and start an investigation, but, I don't know."

In frustration, Haywood slams his hand on his leg and says, "This Saturday, three days from now, when I call to tell you that the missiles have reached Turkey, what are you going to do?"

"If I have to, I'm going to go after a senator."

Chapter 55

Barbara walks into the room in the oncology ward of the UCLA Ronald Reagan Medical Center, near the complete opposite end of the prodigious and world-renowned facility that she normally prowls. The tag on the door of the room says that the occupant is a Miss Elvira Peabody. Amazingly, Miss Peabody very closely resembles a recent transfer from Mississippi. She smiles broadly at her patient and asks, "How do you feel."

Uri responds, "I cannot believe my life, my luck. So many times I should have died, but for people like you. Thank you."

Barbara reads the chart and is impressed, "Wow, you recover quickly."

"Can I go home to Sally? It's difficult for her to come here."

"You're a mess still. How is she?"

"Big. My god, I've only been here a year and she's grown and grown."

Barbara leans over and kisses Uri on the forehead, and he responds, saying, "Good lord, don't let Albert see you doing that."

Barbara laughs and smiles, and a man walks up to the

door pushing a wheelchair and says in a South African accent, "Did someone in here call for therapy?"

Barbara reads the chart and says, "Too soon here, check next door."

Malcolm smiles and salutes Barbara with only his index finger and says, "Alright Doc." He leaves the wheelchair close to the door of the room and walks down to the stairwell, opens the door and dials his phone.

Carl is dressed in a tuxedo and seated at a bar in Paris. He is sipping a martini and listening to a diatribe on world politics by the single least qualified person that he has ever heard speak on the subject, the Russian ambassador to France. Also in the small bar are several of the Russian's assistants and a bevy of beautiful young French women, brought in to service the political figures.

Slightly bored, he is relieved when the phone rings and he sees the number. He apologizes to companions and heads for the first quiet place he can find, answering with a simple, "Yes."

Malcolm apologizes, "I'm so sorry sir to interrupt you, sir, but we have found Uri. He's in the UCLA Medical Center."

"Excellent. Good work."

"I believe that they are moving him tomorrow."

Carl thinks, "Tomorrow. Everything is happening tomorrow." He says, "Who is with him in his room?"

Malcolm responds, "No one. Just a doctor. I think she might be married to the large black man."

Disgusted at the concept of interracial marriages, Carl says, "Americans are pigs. Are you armed? How close are your men?"

"Two minutes, no more."

"Can you take him?"

"Yes sir."

"Will it be a risk."

"Limited risk. What about the woman?"

"If she is there, take her. Take her, kill her. Your choice."

"Yes sir."

Carl thinks and says before he hangs up, "The opera starts in less than an hour. Let me know what happens."

"Yes sir."

The phone clicks dead. Malcolm dials his phone and says curtly, "Bob and Norman to the Oncology ward level 5 and you bring the Suburban to the front."

Malcolm checks his watch and steps toward the door at the end of the corridor. He screws the suppressor onto the barrel of his trusty Berreta PX4 Storm. He then peeks through the door and waits. After a few minutes, the elevator door opens and two men in orderly smocks walk into the corridor. Malcolm walks out to meet them and whispers, "Bob, you hold the elevator, and Norman, you come with me."

Peering into the room, Norman glances at the name tag on the door reading "Elvira Peabody" and makes a quizzical face. Malcolm steps through the door with his suppressed pistol raised to shoulder height aimed at Uri. Just then a shot is fired over Malcolm's head and he ducks out of the way. "SHIT!"

Behind him, hearing the gunshot, the nurses scatter as one reaches to the post nine eleven alarm, lifts the cover and presses the button. The alarm sounds and the entire building is alerted.

Malcolm peeks around the corner and sees that the bed is now empty. Uri has crawled out of the bed and has taken cover behind a small couch. Only the pistol can be seen, which barks again and the door jam directly over Malcolm's head explodes into splinters.As Malcolm turns to leave, he sees the Barbara with a clipboard, running into the corridor from around the corner. As she passes the elevator, Malcolm yells, "Grab her!"

Surprised, she stops directly in front of Bob, who is holding the elevator. Bob reaches for her, and Barbara turns around and backs directly into Norman coming up from behind her. She freezes, feeling the cold steel in her back. Norman looks over his shoulder at Malcolm and asks, "Kill her or bring her?"

The color washes completely out of Barbara's face as

she hears Norman speak. She steels herself and spins with the clipboard turned sideways as her weapon and nails Norman in the face with the edge of the clipboard. In shock and surprise, Norman discharges his unsuppressed weapon and the noise reverberates in the corridor. Barbara, with a look of complete alarm, sinks to the floor clutching a gaping wound in her side.

Malcolm, resigned to failure, pulls Norman into the elevator and presses the ground floor button. Bob, behind him asks rhetorically, "Who gives a patient in a hospital a fucking loaded gun? Was she the one married to the kaffer?" Malcolm, still thinking nods in the affirmative. Bob continues, "Then we did her a favor, eh?"

Norman and Bob laugh cruelly while Malcolm somberly considers what he will tell Carl.

Chapter 56

Carl is seated in his personal box on the opening night of the Paris Opera, next to two beautiful young women and the Russian ambassador. They are awaiting the opening curtain. Carl feels the vibration of his phone and looks around before answering. Seeing that everyone appears to be preoccupied with their own business, he excuses himself, stands and answers with a quiet, "Yes."

Malcolm gets directly to the point, "The target had a gun and fired the first shot."

"A gun in the hospital? Did you get him?"

"No."

"Did you kill him?"

"No, sir."

"Did you at least kill the doctor?"

Silence on the line, and after a count Malcolm answers, "She took a bullet from extreme close range in the torso. But she is in the hospital when she was shot, so I would say possibly. Severely injured but alive when we left."

The lights of the opera house start to dim and the orchestra starts, letting people get to their seats. Carl contemplates his next act and gets up and steps through the opening next to his private seat and says, "Report to

Demitre, now!" Carl hangs up the phone and instantly dials Demitre's number. Before Demitre can speak, Carl orders him, "Find them and protect the delivery. Then, when finished, see that they are all dead, including the good doctor who is in the hospital with a bullet wound. Clear?" Carl looks around hastily and sees that no one was listening.

Demitre responds with a simple, "Yes, sir."

FRIDAY MORNING

Alone in the waiting room, Albert appears almost comical trying to sleep on the tiny sofa. He is woken by the sound of the door opening, and he jumps up defensively, although sleepily, to his feet only to see Haywood and Justin entering the room. He wraps his big arms around them both and sobs, "She's so weak. I'm so afraid."

Justin asks, "Where is Evelyn?"

Albert looks behind him and says, "She was right there a second ago. I couldn't keep my eyes open."

Haywood shakes his head, "Today, where ever you are, you need to be armed. When this is over, they are coming to finish this." Albert looks with sudden realization as Haywood continues. "Big Jim has a vest and some hide-able weapons back at Evan's house. We're meeting over there; want us to bring you some?"

Justin says, still hugging Albert, "Tune up sucker, we're

getting the band back together."

Albert looks at him and sees that Justin has that glint in his eye. "Damn, Justin. That's right. We're going back to war. We didn't call this one, this one called us. I'm not staying here, the war is out there. "

Haywood stands in his way and asks, "You sure?"

Albert steels himself and says, "These are not people you can run from or wait for, at least if you want to walk away at the end. We take the fight to them. Is Uri safe?"

Haywood finds a smile in his answer and points over his shoulder with his thumb, "That bad boy is out in the hallway."

Albert sticks his head out in the doorway in the dim light of early morning and sees only a man wrapped head to foot in gauze wrap with a blanket covering his arms and legs. Uri raises the blanket slightly, showing one of those Israeli automatic pistols that Big Jim was so proud of. Evelyn walks toward them from the restrooms. She sees the grim look on them all and says, "Haywood, I trust you. But you have to take care of my Justin. I don't know what you have to do. But I know you have to do it. I called Cherry and the girls are all coming down here with guns in their purses. We're going to shoot anybody we don't recognize and a couple we do." She turns and heads toward Uri and waves at him, "You OK sweetie?" The Mummy waves back.

Haywood stops just short of intending to tell her what to

do, realizing that it was their choice. He also realizes he is starting to become OK with it. So he completely changes his demeanor and says, "This is nuts, but since this is what it is, Margaret used to be a crack shot. You take care of my baby for me and let her pick the targets."

"We decided on shifts," Evelyn continues, "Margaret with Mary and the cops are nervous, so if we can get a 2-minute warning." She looks at her husband, Justin, and asks, "Please? You know what you need to do. Look into the future, see what they are planning and get out of the way."

Justin looks confused, and Albert grabs him. Albert says, "I know what she means, you see stuff and it comes true. We know you can't really see the future, but you see stuff none-the-less."

Justin, caught up in the emotions, says, "I will do what I can. I think Ernie is working for them. He knows where some of us live, so none of us can go home. I'll monitor the video feeds I forced you guys to put in."

Haywood suggests, "Then let's put this plan in motion. Starting at Evan's with the rest of em."

Evan looks at Haywood and asks, "We do have a plan, don't we?"

Chapter 57

Demitre awoke as the first breath of light kissed the western sky. However, because all the nicer hotel rooms near the beach in southern California face west, you wouldn't be able to tell. Coffee was wheeled into Demitre's room by the excellent service staff at the Fairmont, famous for their coffee and breakfast treats.

The certainty in Demitre's mind was tempered by the knowledge that his main adversaries in the day's quest possessed an unusual amount of dumb luck. Training, education and hard work always trumped dumb luck in the long run, but the long run as of today was over and there was only the short term. Here, certainty, if at all attainable, was to be found in the planning.

The location of the missiles was top secret. But everyone involved knew that they were located at a test area at the 29 Palms Marine Air Field test center. The switch had already been made. The missiles had been mixed into the regular run of test equipment set for normal delivery. All that was left to do, was take it to the drop off in Los Angeles.

So close to completion, Demitre simply had to determine which road to take to limit his risks. He listed his adversaries, both real and potential; Haywood; the four idiots with the dumb luck; probably Ernie, and then Malcolm and the members of his fire team as the last type of enemy. The last type were the ones he could use until the job was done and then they would certainly turn on him. His own team being at risk did not set well. Although the team he had assembled were not family, they were none-the-less loyal comrades. Demitre felt bad that he was being forced to place them at risk. If possible he would compensate. If possible.

Demitre switched gears and began thinking about the shipping trucks. Some sort of subterfuge would be played out, some form of attack would occur, of that he was certain. With Haywood discredited, it would probably be left to the four idiots and what ever help they could muster. He would not take them lightly, he had already made that error. A simple plan was always best. One of two drivers, the second a decoy, would stop at the rustic post office down the street from Pappy and Harriet's in the tiny hamlet of Pioneertown, California, the other at C & S Coffee Shop in Yucca. As both ambushes were already in place, he simple had to decide which truck went where, then off to LA.

That those idiots from Ardberg had already been ripped off was their own fault. That fact would not be discovered for days, and the missiles would be long gone. The shipping trucks had been planned and listed to enter and exit the base months ahead, so as not to raise the unnecessary suspicion of a last-minute event. Demitre knew he just had to pick the best ambush point, and he was leaning toward the tiny Pioneertown post office as the final ambush point. It was more remote and seldom even open in the afternoon. The decision to kill both drivers would be his own. It was the safest way. Both would have seen his face, ergo, both would have to die. They, unlike his men, were not family. Take out the first driver outside the tiny post office and the second in LA when the missiles were delivered.

Ernie was a different problem. Demitre would probably not be able to talk him into making himself available after trying to kill him twice already. The risk during the current run that Ernie posed, however, was probably low. He would have to be dealt with later though.

Then there was Carl, the enigma. On the surface, a powerful man, friend to the leaders and future leaders of the world. Underneath, a treacherous scoundrel with a reputation for making people taste their own testicles before they die painfully. Carl was flawed by his enormous ego. Not incapable of planning, but incapable of thinking anyone could outwit him. The flaw in Demitre's plan, admitted or not, would always be that Carl would spare no expense in hunting him down and ferreting him out to exact his quite literal pound of flesh. Well, more than a pound. Carl's own personal success or failure was no longer material to him.

His vast wealth allowed him to repeatedly fail, so long as occasionally he did receive the big payoff.

Carl's underworld activities were like a roulette wheel, except on this wheel, planning at least partly replaces luck. Investing in several jobs at the same time with enormous potential payoffs with the real expectation of at least one "hitting" and actually paying off. Demitre knew that he was merely a chip on the betting line. Win or loose, the tiny chip wagered would be forgotten. That was Demitre's hope, albeit unrealistic, that he be forgotten. To slip away with his paltry winnings, at least enough for his modest design. The payoff for Carl in this endeavor should be near a hundred million dollars. At the same time, Carl may have other pots boiling in other parts of the world. How to get away? That is the riddle.

Resignedly, Demitre dials his cell phone, knowing full well what time it is in the South of France, and without the least bit of surprise, the phone is answered almost before it rings. Carl's voice has the tiniest bit of apprehension in it as he says, "Yes?"

Demitre starts in, "We are now ready."

Carl asks transparently, "Where will Malcolm and his men be?"

Demitre thinks, "Yes, he will be in position to strike", but instead he says, "He will be with me, in case there is a problem with the actual shipment, his men will be my reserve and personal guard."

Carl relaxes and decides he must call Malcolm now to confirm his good fortune but asks, "What about the others?"

"Malcolm has been instructed what to do. We believe we know where the women will be hidden, and that will be done as we go to finish Uri."

Carl asks, "Which route will be the actual route?"

Demitre hesitates revealing anything that could potentially get out, but he tells him anyway, saying, "The Cafe in Yucca Valley. I decided that lots of witnesses would be best. That way, if Haywood and the others show up at all, we would have the exits protected and they would not be able to get away. They can be dealt with, and the weapons will be most of the way to their destination when the smoke clears." Then Demitre states a truth, "I am assuming that they know everything."

Carl considers and replies, "For planning purposes, that is always the safest."

Demitre struggles to maintain his composure, "No. I mean I assume that their intel is better than yours and they actually know everything."

"How is that possible?"

"The logistics man at the factory, the idiot at MGM. Too many loose ends."

Carl reflects, "Will the shipment get through?"

"If they don't know it, or ferret out the trap, otherwise,..."

He trails off.

Carl is getting upset, "I spent over $5 million setting this up."

Again, Demitre thinks, but does not say, "And heard nothing I said." What he does say is, "We should kill all of them and start over. I will make it work."

Carl says, "We have too much invested; we will do it. You *will* do it." and he I clicks off the phone.

Chapter 58

Just after sunrise on a different western-facing beach, another group is meeting. This one is slightly larger than anticipated by the regulars in the room. Along the entrance is a stack of prototype "Sandia" body armor and a broad variety of weaponry. The group consists of the four, Haywood, Big Jim and two of his investigators, Cardozo and Drescher, primed for some action.

Haywood is concerned and starts by telling the men, "We are going to have to react to them. Which means that our ability to plan is limited, and that means you are at risk. We are at risk. We have certain inside information and as always we can thank Justin for it. That is why Justin is not going with us today." Before Justin can protest, Haywood holds up his hand to prevent him from speaking and continues, "We, the rest of us are safest if you're at your computers. We love you, but you are not allowed to get into the pool. The rest of us," he looks around the room, "are a conglomeration of citizenry. Three of us over age sixty, a couple of hillbillies,..." Big Jim nudges his two detectives and whispers so everyone can hear, "That would be you two losers." Robert, grateful for the break in tension, laughs a brief responsive laugh and stops apologetically. Haywood smiles with his eyes and continues, "or would you prefer, Crackers?"

Drescher raises his hand and offers pressing his southern drawl to the max, "'Rednecks, would be fine, Mr. Haywood, Sir," and the light moment is a great relief to the group.

Haywood continues, "Justin again, has discovered that they have two alternate courses," He points to a map showing the Yucca Valley and 29 Palms area. "Both are within 5 miles of each other, but it's 12 long minutes on the road. They will have more men, younger, better trained and the appearance of authority because they will be driving the truck." Evan snickers at the absurdity of the comment, so Haywood retorts, "Which is more important than you might think. If they call the police or the Marines, We look like the truck thieves."

Robert asks, "How is that possible? We're trying to stop the terrorists."

Big Jim chimes in, "But true none-the-less. We are all alone. Haywood tried to get the FBI involved, but his credibility had been ruined. We're it! The good news is we don't have to win, we just need to stop them from getting the trucks away."

Albert asks, "Why would they not just drive straight through?"

Haywood shrugs but responds, "Not completely sure.

Partly to confuse us about a trap, I guess. Partly because that's what most of the noon drivers do. Hit the road and eat after loading."

Haywood says, "I updated all the information to my old boss at the FBI, but I don't know if we can count on any help." He pauses, drawing their attention back to the map. "The two locations we are concerned about are a tiny hardly used post office in downtown Pioneertown and a coffee shop in Yucca Valley. If it was me, I would do some kind of an exchange of drivers to give them some level of an alibi. Knowing Demitre the way we do, I expect him to kill anyone that has seen his face. So they are expendable." He looks at his friends grimly, "If I was doing it, I would use two trucks, so we are planned for both. Our fallback plan is to slow them down and make enough of a spectacle that someone comes to check. Then we tell them what we believe is transpiring and try to limit the credibility of the driver. *No heroics!* Got it?"

Big jim stands and claps Haywood on the back, "My rednecks and me brung some hardware. The problem will be Albert and me as they don't make this equipment in our size." The room briefly giggles at the remark briefly as he continues, "The weapons are not loaded, so if you reach for something you are not used to, try it out first, OK?"

The group heads to the table, and the grim reality of what they are walking into hits them broadside. The Sandia body armor is waist to neck wrist to shoulder. It was designed for the people who sat up on the top of the Humvee's weapons turret in Iraq. A kevlar-based, woven and reinforced structure that was very good but not fool proof. The armor is a significant improvement over the casual shirts and jackets they are currently wearing.

Haywood again raises his hand to speak, "Does anybody have any fucking idea why we're doing this?" Everyone laughs briefly. "You are my friends and I want you all safe. To that end, Big Jim is in command of C&S Coffee Shop and I am in charge of Pioneertown. I have a couple of surprises, depending on which location, that call for an ambush of any of them stupid enough to be outside. And, I can't believe they will expect the kevlar. But I will remind you that it will do nothing about a head or leg shot."

Robert adds, "Or a weenie shot, so protect your cookies."

Again laughter, and Haywood continues, "Or a weenie shot as that noisy asshole in the corner pointed out." Robert curtsies gracefully. "If we wear helmets, they will change their shooting patterns to adjust expecting vests, so we are taking certain risks with your lives here. Do you hear us?" He has everyone's attention and continues, "So move fast and don't get shot!"

Chapter 59

Uri had insisted on extra gauze and pads and extra tight tape today underneath his mummy costume, realizing that he will probably need to move around way more than anyone with good sense would allow. But he knows that if the bad guys come here early, he is the last line of defense for the five women who will be in the hospital with him. No matter what else, he must protect his friends.

Expecting the worst, but relatively certain they are safe until nearer to five o'clock this afternoon, he ignores the body armor that Big Jim dropped off and checks the fully restored HK automatic rifle and two Berreta pistols. Jim elected to give Uri the HK because he knew Uri could hit anything with that. He left the two Berreta pistols because Uri was severely wounded and, well, he would probably be dealing with extreme close range.

Refusing the pain killers, Uri knew he was in for a rough day. But better to be clear headed and in pain than miss something at a time when his friends that would surely need his best performance.

Surprisingly hungry, Uri ate everything on the plate. The ancient fables about the blandness of hospital food simply didn't apply in the UCLA Medical Center. Or maybe Barbara had control over that too. Uri smiled and reflected on the fact that he didn't put that past her.

His thoughts turned to Sally. He was immensely relieved to think that of all of the people he cherished, she was probably the most safe. He none-the-less longed to see her, knowing that his life was on the line. He quickly disregarded that act of selfishness and got to the task at hand. "How best to protect those at risk'. This was his gift, despite his early years of putting people at risk. He was an efficient strategist. Uri could look around him and know instinctively the best or worst elements of his surrounding. Uri could know how to set the best trap, and today the people that would come for them would definitely use the best weaponry and have a backup plan. Planning leads to execution. Perfect planning leads to perfect execution. So the first element would be to select the most defensible location, not necessarily the most hidden. Accessible to aid by way of campus or city police, preferably where an assault would be easy for assistance to surround.

Uri fully realizes that a suicide mission is possible though not likely. A suicide mission is something for which little realistic preparation can be done. What could be done had been done after nine eleven. Alarms and deterrents aside, a dedicated person willing to give up his life was hard to stop.

Down the corridor from his position at one of the major

intersections on the ward, Uri's four "charges" for the day appear and his demeanor softens completely, "Ladies. Welcome to my den of iniquity."

Evelyn smiles and retorts, "You wish!" as she vamps into the room bringing giggles from the other three.

Uri asks, "How is Barbara?"

Margaret replies, "They stopped the sepsis and no vital organs were hit; she's awake and ordering everyone around, so the nurses are afraid to go in her room." Uri smiles, and Margaret asks, "Are you up for this?"

Uri touches her hand and assures her, "In my shallow and unfulfilled life, I was first a killer of men and second a protector of innocence. Today, you are my life. If your husbands were available, they would be in my place. Because they're all occupied with what I should be doing, I will offer all that I am." Afraid he has been too serious, he adds, "First let's be clear. The plan is to find a place, and if they do come, to stay out of the way and call backup. So, do I think I can hit the alarm and duck? Yes, I think I can do that." The four women smile at him,. and he hopes that he was a decent enough liar that they would feel comforted. Now, he just had to act strong. The situation is complicated by the fact that they will have to push his wheelchair and wheel him to where they were going.

He looks out at the trusting faces and says, "Let's go get Barbara then."

Evelyn retorts, "She's my sister, so I know firsthand that she's a monster when she's injured. So I can say we absolutely need to get a tranquilizer dart and knock her ass out or suffer a worse fate ourselves!" The rest laugh at the respite of the light moment.

Chapter 60

Haywood is seated in the back of Evan's latest monster Humvee, deep in thought and filled with concern about his and his friends lives. He feels a buzzing from his belt and almost answers the phone before he realizes that it may be a call to Ernie. It turns out that the call is to Ernie. As soon as he sees that the call has been taken, Haywood presses to be connected and hears Demitre say, "Ernie, I am intentionally keeping your name out of the conversation, so I would expect some form of compensation from you in return."

"I don't know how I'm getting paid yet, do I? So you want me to what exactly?"

Demitre continues, "I have transferred the funds to an account in your name. What I need from you is protection. I need to know if anybody is coming for me."

Ernie retorts, "That is supposed to make me feel comfortable. Did you know that your boss had a hit put on a doctor at UCLA Medical Center yesterday? Do you think you're in charge of anything anymore?"

"The game has changed. Trust me, that's why I'm leaving your name out of it."

"You say that..."

At this very moment, Haywood cuts in and asks, "What if I could offer you both a way out?" knowing he was taking a horrible risk in losing his best source of information and acting against 40 years of training and experience. Albert nodding off in the front passenger seat, opens his eyes to look at Haywood with alarm. Evan is driving and hears nothing, but he notices Albert's concerned expression.

Ernie, secretly guessing who it is, says nothing as Demitre asks, "Who is this?"

Haywood responds, "Samuel Haywood. I assume you've heard of me?"

After a moment of silence, Demitre asks Ernie, "Mr. Alvarez, you know what this means to your money."

Ernie responds, "Wait."

As Haywood says, "You know he didn't invite us, Demitre. And who says I'm speaking to you. You tried to kill some friends of mine."

Ernie responds, "Their computer guy must of done this, not me!"

Haywood senses the matter falling apart and says again, "Seriously, what if I have a way that both of you can get out? Demitre, we both know what Carl is going to do to you win or lose when this is done."

Demitre, taking the bait, asks, "And how can you prevent me from getting dead?"

Haywood reels him in, "First you tell me when and

where is the ambush. The post office or the cafe?"

Demitre, reeling from the concept that his enemy already knew about the locations and the ambush, responds, "Not so fast, Mr. Haywood. What would I get from you? A life in prison?"

Ernie is listening carefully knowing his life is also in the balance. Demitre continues, "I don't do prison. If I can't come out with cash and a get-out-of-jail-free, I'm not interested."

Haywood responds, "Ernie, do you remember what we talked about before/"

"Sort of, we talked about maybe, you were going to fake my death?"

"How about if Demitre shoots you and we shoot Demitre in front of an audience of Carl's other goons?"

Demitre responds, "Too many things can go wrong. Like you forget to use fake bullets and do it for real."

Haywood responds, "You thought Uri was dead last year didn't you?"

Demitre responds, "Until that idiot contacted Milkoff to try to make a deal."

Haywood smiles, "So which one of you would try to call Carl to make a deal and believe he would do differently?"

Ernie waits for Demitre, knowing what his position is already. Demitre responds, "Can I think about it?"

Haywood offers, "You have until one of my friends die.

Ernie, do you trust Demitre?"

Ernie fires back, Hell no. He's tried to kill me twice."

Haywood asks, "Which would you rather have, Mr. Alvarez? Demitre shoot blanks knowing we'll give him up to Carl if he screws up? Or let the normal course take place and have that other idiot from South Africa, hound you to the ends of the earth and shoot you with real bullets?" The silence in the Humvee is complete as Albert and Evan, having pulled off to the side of the road, are staring holes through Haywood.

Demitre asks, "We keep what we can salvage money-wise and you don't send us to prison?" Ernie leans in waiting for the answer.

Haywood asks, "What do you think is important to me? My friends live, the missiles get stopped. I just never want to see either one of you again. Clear?"

Demitre responds, "I do not control the situation as much as you may believe."

Haywood responds, "Carl will turn everyone over to that South African asshole?"

"Exactly."

Haywood pauses and then asks, "Well doesn't it seem like a healthy choice to you both?"

Ernie anxiously awaits Demitre's response but then blurts out, "Demitre. You know I can't unless you do, and you know Carl blames you for his own poor planning."

Demitre pauses before he asks, "You think the bigots from South Africa will just go away?"

Haywood responds, "You need them to be alive long enough to report to Carl and then you don't care. Everyone thinks your dead and Carl becomes Malcolm's problem."

Chapter 61

Doing the math, it became eminently clear that Demitre had not achieved his ultimate financial goal. He had shaved close to a million dollars from the funds that Carl had established to capitalize the project. He was under budget, as far as he was concerned, so the funds were like a bonus. Besides, Carl had tossed extra crap into the deal like that devil, Uri. And before that, Carl had hired Lloyd, despite Demitre's protest that, "Lloyd was only concerned about Lloyd." It simply didn't make sense to hire someone that wasn't afraid of you.

Demitre, doing the quick calculations, first the $2.1million or so from that idiot from Ardberg, Mr. Jenkins. Less, of course, the $400,000.00 since it appeared he might actually have to pay Ernie. Plus the nest egg he had been able to squeeze out of those pompous idiots in Moscow. He was still short of his $10 Million retirement goal by almost a third. Demitre sighed and responded aloud to himself, "But I'm still alive. A consummation devoutly to be wished." Then his thoughts drifted to that sweet house in Venice that Mr. Jenkins had paid off. Then shrugged to himself, "No. Maybe not. Too greedy."

The math that Ernie was was using was infinitely more simple. With barely $200 from the ten grand in the envelope with the tiny GPS device was all he had left. The $400,000.00 was a windfall more than he could hope for, and it was in an account he could access. Ernie really wished he had paid more attention to Justin when he had explained how to transfer cash without leaving a trail. $400,000.00, or less if he would have to deal with laundering it himself, or, maybe he could, ...

In his man cave with eight glowing monitors feeding him information, Justin is ready. He would never be able to fully explain how he had hooked up the satellite linkage without his friends knowing he had violated beaucoup federal regulations, but he now had a closeup view of the action if it occurred at the post office in the tiny burg of Pioneertown. The good side was if there were hidden perps, he would be able to switch to infrared and scope them out. The prospect of watching his friends die like in a scene on Television, was something he tried repeatedly to force from his mind.

Pioneertown was a logical location for all sides. It wasn't directly between the missiles and the Ardberg factory in Pasadena, but it was a regular stop for the drivers, because of the food, and it was only four miles out of the way. More importantly from Haywood's perspective, there was some comfort to be found in familiarity with the turf, because they had friends in Pioneertown,

Justin's main conflict was two-fold. First, he wasn't with his friends. But he would make the best of the situation and do all that he could from here, which he acknowledged might be a lot. Second, he had trusted Ernie, but Ernie had betrayed them and gone over to the dark side. No telling how much personal information he had given over. The new security cameras at everyone's house were motion activating, so he would know immediately if they were assaulted. But still, while inside their confidence, he had killed a man. True, he would not be missed by any of them, but it was simply not his choice.

Justin's phone rings. Recognizing the number, he is stumped but answers anyway, "Killer, you call to gloat about your new job?"

"I work for Agent Haywood now. So does Demitre."

"Bullshit, you work for yourself."

"True, but you know Haywood is listening, so you judge me later. I never let anyone know I was at your house, or Evan's. They thought I was working by myself."

"As if."

Haywood, listening in, chips in, "Justin, take a breath. Let him speak."

Ernie starts, "I will trade the channels of the bad guys' radio receivers for Justin's help transferring the cash from an account so it can't be traced. Then if I screw up, you can take the money back."

"Dude, we have satellite hookup, we don't need..."

Haywood interrupts, "Justin, do it. We know what they are saying to each other we are way ahead of the game."

Justing replies, "Which they'll change as soon as they realize that they have been compromised."

Ernie asks, "You got a satellite?"

Justin is still pissed and does not respond but asks Haywood, "If I do it, that's okay with you?"

Haywood responds, "Do it and send us the satellite feed, OK. Now deal with it. Oh, then call back, I have new information."

Chapter 62

Big Jim, riding uncomfortably in the large rental car jokes, "We should'a got that Humvee. I could'a been comfortable at least." His radio clicks on, and Haywood says, "Big Jim? Over."

Big Jim hits his com link and responds, "Hey sucker, I hope you're comfortable. We got this little shit rental."

"I have something else. Are you almost there?"

"Pulling into the cafe now."

"OK, you get the real missiles, but that doesn't mean there won't be a fight. Squawk the three frequencies I'm texting you and find the bad guys. We're sending satellite imaging, so we should be able to spot the little bastards if they're hiding. Roger?"

"Satellites, enemy radio frequencies, you boy's surely don't play fair."

Haywood grins at Albert next to him and responds, "Fair enough. Don't use 'em hillbilly. Remember, these boys never saw "Deliverance', so they don't know what to be afraid of with you rednecks."

"OK. We're at the cafe. Should we just walking order food, or what?"

Justin, listening in, adds, "Infrared signature across the

street. Anybody see it?"

Cardozo keys, "Where?"

Justin replies, "Can't tell elevation from 15 miles in the air, sorry."

Drescher replies, "Why, is it broken?"

Everyone rolls their eyes at the intentionally dumb reply. Big Jim shuts it down saying, "OK, game faces, we're there."

Haywood keys his mike and says, "They have a pretty good Eggs, sausage and pancakes special."

Cardozo replies as they get out of the car and walk toward the restaurant door past the medium-sized truck parked in the lot. "I'm hungry! What happens if this is the trap?"

Haywood says, "Then duck. Fair enough?"

Justin continues, "Do you mind? Can I continue?" Silence from the rest. "OK, One on the roof next door to the cafe, three in the closed restaurant across the street and one on the roof across the side street is five. One too many?"

Haywood whispers in his com link as he approaches the turn off to the post office, "Well, it looks as though Demitre's at your party." Then clicks off the line starting to look for potential hiding places around the post office.

Albert looks over and smiles, wondering, "So should this actually be called a party or not."

Haywood apologizes, "Probably a bad choice of words. Do you see the truck yet?"

Albert responds, "Nothing here but us chickens."

From the window of the closed Las Palmas restaurant across the street from the C & S coffee shop, Malcolm asks, looking at Big Jim entering the cafe, "Is that the big guy from Mississippi?"

Demitre surmises, "I don't know, but that would be an excellent assumption to work from. That makes those other two hot also. Stay off the radios, OK. Call it a hunch."

Malcolm is concerned at the idea of not giving the information to his men but has to settle for locking eyes with Henry beside him, and he nods for him to go signal the other two men. As Henry steps outside, the man on the roof across from them holds up one finger and Henry responds with hand signals indicating that the last three men entering the restaurant should be considered potential shooters. The man on the roof points to his com unit, and Henry cuts a finger across his throat and then shrugs the universal, "I don't know" signal.

The tiny post office appears to have been thrust into a modern century from some far remote area of the old west. The town as a whole started as a live-in, Old West motion picture set, built in the 1940s. The movie set was designed to provide a place for the actors to live and at the same time to have their homes used as part of the movie set. A number of Westerns and early television shows were filmed in Pioneertown. Roy Rogers was among the original developers and investors, and Gene Autry was a frequent visitor on business and otherwise.

From nearly 500 miles, the satellite view is somewhat more revealing for strategic purposes. The infrared shot quickly exposes the six men stationed strategically around the post office maximizing the crossfire angles and use of camouflage and natural cover. As Justin sends the live satellite feed directly to each of their smart phones, their civilian humvee pulls up to the post office. The casualness they all show as they hop from vehicle, belies the underlying fear each feels at the risk being taken. As huge as Albert is across the shoulders, the body armor makes almost no difference in his overall appearance. Haywood, Robert and Evan all look heavier, but only to people that would otherwise know what they looked like.

From the side of the hill, a mere 100 feet away, Pavel,

one of the shooters, recognizes two of the men from Mississippi and signals the others that those are the men. The bead of his HK automatic rifle follows Haywood dead center mid torso, as Pavel remembers his own injury and the death of his good friend and comrade caused by that man. Eliminate the best shooter is rule one. However, from outward appearances, neither is carrying any weapon. He also remembers the giant black man standing on the porch with shots landing all around him while trying to protect several women. Pavel would never intend to shoot at the women, but when someone is trying to shoot him and women happen to be where the bullets were coming from, then the women had better take cover.

Chapter 63

The 29-foot white Ford truck with a white box labeled "Pollard Transport", turns from the paved area of Pioneertown Road onto the 150-foot stretch of dirt extending from the paved area to the post office. The driver observes an odd conglomerate of men in front of the post office. Several of the men are older, one is short, barely five foot six or seven; and one is a large black man who looks like a 40-year-old bodybuilder. He had been advised to expect only one person. But since he wasn't exactly sure why he was supposed to stop, he would follow orders, as he usually would do. Regardless, he could really use the money, so he wouldn't cause trouble.

Expecting that the deal is a bit shady, he knows the way to impress this employer is to do what he is told and keep his mouth shut. No problem. But still, who are all these people? Per his instructions, he hops out of the cab and walks over to the group and asks, "Who's Tyler? I'm supposed to ask for Tyler."

Outside the C & S coffee shop in Yucca Valley, an exact replica of the truck at the Post Office rolls through a green light and comes to a stop in front of the coffee shop. Matt, the driver, knows perfectly well what is going on. He looks into the window of the closed and dark restaurant across the street and touches his forehead, expecting no return signal. He hops out and walks toward the coffee shop. Malcolm yells into his mouth piece, "Get back into the truck and drive to LA. They're inside the coffee shop."

Demitre looks at Malcolm with shock on his face as Matt turns around and walks back to the cab of the truck. "What have you done?" He keys his mike and yells to his men at the post office, "Now, do it. Spring the trap!"

At the post office, the only one that doesn't hear Demitre's voice is the driver of the truck. All others, from both sides, are listening to Demitre's frequency. The result is that Haywood, Albert, Robert and Evan dive behind the truck to a position of comparative safety. The raking of automatic fire from three different directions shreds the side of the truck, the front of the post office and the unfortunate driver. Albert falls behind Haywood hard, and Haywood asks, "You OK?

Albert responds, Yeah, I just tripped. Robert? Evan? You guys OK?"

Robert asks pleadingly, "Are we going to shoot back?"

Haywood ducks from a shot fired and yells, "Heads

down guys! We're out-gunned and they have position on us."

From the hillside, the six trained shooters do as they are told and wonder as they start shooting the logical question, "Why did they jump out of the way at the same time we are told to shoot?" Pavel, realizing something is up, stops shooting and hears the others also stopping. He considers pulling the ear plugs from his ears so he can hear, but fortunately for him, he doesn't get around to it. Although he would have heard the "fluke, fluke, fluke" sound of the mortar-like launcher firing three rounds in rapid succession, he would never have heard another thing thereafter his entire life. The launcher, which is normally used at the Marine training center when they wanted to simulate an actual attack, fired three rounds directly over the heads of the six men on the hillside. The three rounds, although one would probably have been enough, were placed so that they would each explode 50 feet directly over the pairs of shooters. The rounds, although not normal military ordinance, would be considered an industrial-strength substitute for hand-tossed "flash bang" grenade.

Four miles away, at the cafe, the five men with the matching ear pieces dig into their ears like badgers pulling out the ear pieces as the massive decibel burst occurs. Almost as quickly as the earpieces are out, the 8-second time delay of the actual sound from the tiny post office reaches the coffee shop like rolling thunder. Across the street, the three men inside Las Palmas Restaurant look at each other and know absolutely that the trap has gone horribly wrong. In front of them, they learn that the rest of the plan has also gone asunder, as four shinny new California Highway Patrol cars pull up and block all exits for the truck front and back.

Demitre offers to Malcolm, "You might tell your men to drop their guns and walk directly away from everything, and we can pick them up a couple blocks away." Malcolm looks back at Henry, who shrugs, and Malcolm turns back to Demitre, keys his com link and says, "Drop your weapons where you are and walk directly away from the truck. We will pick you up at a two-block perimeter. Out. Stay off the com line."

Chapter 64

Outside the post office, the six stunned and defeated men stagger to their feet as a mere result of their proximity to the blast. The size of the blast from a distance of 50-feet was more devastating than people would generally realize. Normal ordinance is designed to do many different things. Anti-personnel shells contain shrapnel and are designed to explode in mid-air, so their fragments will spread over a large area. Armor-piercing ammunition tends to be hard, sharp, and narrow, often with lubrication of some kind. Incendiary projectiles include a material such as white phosphorus, which burns fiercely. The sole function of these rounds was specifically to scare Marines in a training format, intended to be as close to actual combat as possible without lethal fire. They would be more closely compared to fireworks that would set off the alarms of cars parked in the area, just bigger.

Despite their non-lethal intentions, the blast of the three projectiles are completely disorienting as well as deafening. Five of the six would-be shooters stand without their weapons and are pointed approximately at a 90-degree angle to the post office and do not in any way appear dangerous. The sixth man stands with his gun at the ready but is pointed back toward the hills in the opposite direction. Haywood signals for the other three men to approach and secure the five, as he keeps a bead on the sixth man all the way up to him. As he reaches the man, Pavel lowers his his weapon to his side and Haywood kicks the gun from his hand. The six men are cuffed with long tie-wraps, their headsets are removed and they are guided like sheep back toward the truck.

Then Butch St. Mark, a local man in his fifties, wearing jeans, a brown chambray shirt and a California Angels cap, walks up and waves to Haywood. Albert sees him and says, jokingly, "I always wanted to say this, You think you used enough dynamite there Butch?"

Robert and Evan laugh as Haywood and Butch look at each other and shake their heads in disbelief. Haywood asks, "Can you believe what I work with?"

Butch answers, "They're your friends." and smiles.

Haywood points at the would be shooters and asks, "How long until they are back to normal?"

Butch responds, "Depends on whether or not they took out their ear pieces. They left them in, they'll be okay in a couple of minutes. If they took them out, they may be deaf forever."

Haywood looks at Robert, Albert and evan and all three hold up the head pieces that they had confiscated. Robert responds for the group, "They all had them in."

Joking, Butch points at the men and asks Haywood, "What you gonna do with them?"

Playing along, Haywood responds with a shrug, "Take 'em out into the dessert with the snakes?" One turns around and looks concerned as Haywood winks and adds, "See, they're starting to come back to already."

Haywood loads them into the back of the truck and reaches for his phone to call the sheriffs office as a sheriff's vehicle drives up and stops. The deputy gets out of the car and walks straight up to Butch, the only one he recognizes and asks, "What the hell happened, Butch?"

Butch starts, "Those guys we put in the truck were hiding up on the hill. I was right over there by my truck trying to figure out what to take out to the base, and they started shooting at the postoffice and killed that guy a minute after he got out of the truck. I dropped a couple rounds of ordinance I was taking out to the training grounds on 'em, and these guys drove up in time to help me tie 'em up."

"Are you shitting me? Holy crap Butch, you could'a killed "em. I heard them bombs go off half way to Yucca."

Butch responds, "Naw, just some flash bangs. I told these guys to hang around to tell you what happened." Pointing at Haywood, "This one here used to be an FBI agent. They said they would stay but that they had to get back into LA. I know how to get in touch; he's a friend of ours from way back."

Haywood offers, "We wrote down our information. Their weapons are where they dropped them when those bombs went off. We heard them and came running over to see what all the noise was."

Albert nods and says, "That was seriously loud."

The sheriff deputy smiles and looks around. "Yeah, I guess you can leave as long as we can find you."

They pile in the car and leave.Haywood puts his earpiece back in and keys, "Justin, you there buddy?"

Justin responds, "Yup. You rolling back to Yucca? Remember you guys have to be back before 5 PM."

Chapter 65

As Haywood and the guys role up to the Coffee shop, Big Jim and the guys walk out of the coffee shop with his deputies and taps one of the highway patrolmen on the shoulder and points at Haywood. "That's him, that's Haywood there."

Haywood walks toward the patrolman and asks, "Can I help you sir?"

"You Haywood?"

"Yes, sir."

"Agent McHugh said we should shut this truck down and ask for you. The driver seems to have slipped away when the cruisers showed up. Should we cut the lock? With him on the run, we have probable cause."

Haywood pauses and decides to come clean. "Not a good idea. The truth is I believe that this truck is carrying a brand new missile that's being sold to the worst kind of terrorists."

The patrolman tries to peer into Haywood's head to see if he is the butt of a huge joke. Sensing this, Haywood adds, "I am dead serious. If I'm correct, and trust me I would just a soon be wrong, the truck could be rigged. Do you have access to X-ray equipment?"

The patrolman asks, "You think it's rigged?" Haywood shrugs as the patrolman gathers the other officers to him and calls their headquarters for instructions.

Haywood retreats to the Humvee and dials McHugh as they pull away from the curb on their way back to LA. McHugh picks up on the first ring asking, "Haywood, you still alive?"

Haywood smiles and offers, "Thanks. I mean it. I had friends that I was concerned about, and all I wanted to do was stop that damn truck."

"You'll be happy to know that I called Mr. Trimble, and he acted like you were a flake."

"Did you agree with him?"

"Well, yes I did. When I asked him what he knew about a truck filled with experimental missiles headed for Turkey, he froze up like a popsicle. So we sent some guys over and picked him up."

Haywood pumps his fist, smiles at his friends and asks, "What about that guy we gave you at Ardberg?"

"Did you know he just paid off his house with foreign money?"

"Well, yes, since I told you that."

"He's in custody, and I think he's going to sing like a canary. In fact, I think the local police are on the way to his house with a search warrant as we speak."

Haywood checks his watch and says, "Boss, you will never know how much I appreciate your help."

"Which reminds me, When I hung up the phone, Trimble waited about two minutes and called Senator Carter's wife. The wife of the very senator that called the hounds on your pension and retirement."

Haywood smiles again as McHugh continues, "Which only proves the old adage that sometimes when everyone else thinks you're acting paranoid, the assholes really are after you."

McHugh asks, "So what are you going to do now?"

Haywood pauses and says, "Protect my friends. That's all I care about now."

"No tricks?"

Haywood responds, "A few."

Chapter 66

Demitre's cell rings, and he grabs it, checking the number. He is seething about Malcolm's blunder, which compromised his comrades lives, "You'd better have good news for me." He glances at Malcolm and says, much calmer, "Yes, OK, 5 pm. He hangs up his phone and looks at Malcolm, "Ernie called. They ordered an ambulance for Uri and that doctor you shot. Upper deck of the parking structure behind the Oncology building." His eyes still smoldering, "Do you think you can remember not to use your com lines this time?"

Malcolm blushes, but the look on his face could fry an egg. He considers his words, knowing he will kill Demitre in a few hours, and says nothing to inflame his future victim. Instead he asks, "What is the plan?"

Demitre smiles smugly and says, "The top level is perfect for us. I only have one request." He looks at Malcolm and continues, "I want to kill Uri, and I have an errand to do first, and since you saw to it that my men were killed, you will have to help me. I need to pick up the computer guy."

Malcolm grabs Demitre's arm and forces him to lock eyes, "If you had told us our coms were compromised..."

Demitre interrupts, "It was a guess. I told you not to use them, didn't I?" Demitre sighs and says, "I wasn't sure until everything fell apart, until I was sure that they had to be listening in. How else is what happened possible?"

Malcolm, still gripping Demitre's arm, asks the same question, "Yes, how could they have known?"

Demitre pulls his arm away and retorts, "None-the-less, if you had listened, they would be alive, or free, if they are not dead."

Malcolm, sorting facts, says, "Jenkins?"

Demitre nods, "He gets off shortly. I think we should talk to him. *If* he has not already disappeared."

Malcolm's phone rings, and he looks at the number with a chill running through his heart. Carl wants his update. "Yes sir."

Carl is dressed in a bath robe and is seated at his desk in his exquisite master suite. There is the sound of a shower running in the back-ground. Carl asks, "How did it go?"

Malcolm responds as matter of factly as possible, "The missiles were detained by the Highway Patrol. They showed up out of nowhere in force and impounded the truck."

Carl instantly stands up., His pulse and blood pressure skyrocket, as beads of sweat begin forming on his brow. He pauses and then says, "Kill Uri and the doctor and shut it down."

Malcolm responds to a dead phone line, "Yes sir, I'll... "

A beautiful young woman wearing nothing at all walks out of the bathroom drying her hair. Carl's eyes soften slightly before they go cold and reptilian as he asks her, "Are you aroused by pain, my darling?"

Demitre waits for Malcolm to say something until Malcolm responds, "He wants Uri and the doctor killed. You can find them?" Demitre simply nods and looks away. Malcolm continues, "Then let's start with Mr. Jenkins."

Demitre says, casual despite knowing what clearly the true meaning of Carl's instructions to Malcolm, "Yes, he's the only one that has actually seen my face." He touches his forehead and says, "Then the computer guy I relied on. If he had been more capable, I might have let him live. Too bad." They all climb into a large Suburban SUV and head back into the city.

In the vehicle, Demitre calls Ernie with his phone on speaker so Malcolm can hear and asks, "Are you finally ready to meet me?"

Ernie, shocked at the phone call responds, "No, I still don't trust you."

Demitre smiles and says, "OK, then can I call you if I need you in the future? I have another big payday coming up. To wrap this up, however, have you been able you locate Mr. Jenkins?"

Ernie pauses and says, "I know that the police were at his house. Is that a significant problem? As for the future, we shall see." Demitre nods to Malcolm.

Demitre hands a piece of paper to the driver and Malcolm nods that the drive should go to the address. Demitre responds, "OK, then I'll call you in a couple of weeks."

Ernie, with some trepidation responds, "OK then," and they hang up.

Demitre looks at Malcolm and says, "First I will call a private security company to call the police to see if they have Mr. Jenkins, then we deal with Mr. Alvarez."

Malcolm smiles, and they drive away.

Chapter 67

Demitre's phone rings as they approach Los Angeles on the 60 Freeway and he shows the phone to Malcolm. The listing on the screen reads, "Daylight Security." Demitre answers, "Hello, Mr. Arnold here."

The voice on the phone responds, "Yes, Mr. Arnold, it would appear that Mr. Jenkins is in the custody of the police. It would appear that he was taken at the same time as a Mr. Trimble, who was actually on staff at Homeland Security."

Demitre, sensing that the security company is now fishing, responds, "What on earth for? Was he a terrorist?"

The response is, "I'm sorry, sir, they were unable to give out that information."

Demitre tries to remain calm on the outside as he disconnects the phone. Malcolm is smiling inside because of Demitre's discomfort. Malcolm asks Demitre, "Was Trimble your guy in Homeland Security?"

Demitre responds smugly, "No, I'm afraid he worked for your employer, Mr. de Bourbon."

Malcolm, unsure of what is happening, takes out his phone and dials his boss.

Carl is still in his master suite. The young woman is back in the bathroom and is crying. He says through the door, "Yes, yes, dear. What do you expect? I asked you before we started." She cries louder, so he answers the phone curtly, "Oui?"

Malcolm starts, "Sir, Demitre just found out that Mr. Trimble is in the custody of the American Homeland Security department. Is that a problem we should deal with?"

Carl attempts to control his anger by balling his fist and releasing it several times until he calms enough to respond. "Please tell Demitre that he will receive his final payment when the rest of the matter is resolved. I will be transferring your funds in the morning as requested. Call me when it is done."

Carl hangs up the phone and puts it in the pocket of his silk robe. Adjusting his robe, he walks toward the bathroom and says in a comforting voice. "I don't know dear, do you still want that job or not? If you're going to act like that, I might have to reconsider."

The girl walks out of the bathroom with her mascara running down her cheeks. On the way to the door, she says, "I'm sorry, you've been very generous and I appreciate your help with the job. Yes, I really want the job." When she reaches the door to the master suite, she doesn't hesitate as she walks out and closes the door.

Carl sits at his desk and dials a number from memory. "Abdul, yes it's Carl. The shipment will be delayed at least a month. Would you be interested in shifting to a different product?" Carl moves from his desk to the door and peeks out. Then walks back to the desk listening to the phone. "The problem is the factory. You know, I'm not absolutely sure they are capable of building the units they were advertising. I wouldn't be surprised if they have to eventually cancel completely."

He sits again and crosses his legs then answers the unheard question. "Yes, I am out quite a bit of money on their promises. Please have Gustav contact me, and we will find something you will be just as happy with."

"Thank you." He hangs up and puts his phone in his pocket. He leans over and turns on his computer, clicking a few keys to open an online bank account. From a piece of paper that reads "Malcolm" on one side, he types an account number and hits enter. He gets up and walks out of the room. Carl reaches for his phone and dials a new number.

A deep male voice answers in Russian, "Da."

"Mr. Potkin, this is Carl. I believe we were introduced by Mr. ... "

He is interrupted by the deep voice, in English with a Russian accent, "Yes sir, I know who you are. I am honored to have you call. How can I help you?"

"Ah, to the point, I have two jobs. I need a security unit in South Africa after this weekend for a cleanup. How many can you get together?"

"Twenty-four hours we can be anywhere in the world with four to eight men. Seventy two hours we can have twenty."

"That's what I wanted to hear. The second job will need special discretion, if you understand me. You have come highly recommended, and I am having trouble finding good help right now."

"It would be my honor to assist you. I will guarantee that we will earn your respect with any job large or small."

"Mr. Potkin, there are no small jobs, only small people."

Chapter 68

Half a block off of Ventura Boulevard, in the hilly part of Los Angeles metropolitan area, is Encino, California. Encino, which loosely means "evergreen" in Spanish, is located in the central portion of the San Fernando Valley. The medium-sized 12-unit apartment building is substandard in many ways. The good news is that it will never freeze and it will never be too hot or too humid, so the construction requirements are somewhat simpler than if it were in Wisconsin or Florida. Good news for a contractor on a budget, bad news for anyone expecting to prevent someone from entering when they are not wanted.

The first indication of a problem for Ernie is the loss of power. Not unheard of in the area, but considering the danger of the moment, he feels naked. Scurrying to gather his belongings and leave as quickly as humanly possible, Ernie closes his new laptop and heads toward the door. Suddenly, a foot is stomped on the door's exterior and the $5 dead bolt breaks like the cheap toy that it is, and the door swings in with a bang. Back lit by the bright late-afternoon sun, the ominous outline of Demitre is silhouetted black against the light. Demitre, seeing that Ernie is not reaching for or clutching a weapon, simply says, "This is a real shit hole, Ernie."

Without moving, Ernie retorts, "You haven't paid me yet have you, asshole?"

Demitre steps forward, and Norman and Henry walk into the bright sunlight behind Demitre as Demitre brings his right hand up in a roundhouse punch, catching Ernie above the left eye. Ernie drops everything in his arms and falls to the floor dazed, now surrounded by the three men.

Ernie weakly says, "I helped you. You owe me."

Norman sneers at the cowering lump and says, "You pussy," and spits on him.

Norman raises his gun at Ernie, and Demitre says calmly, staring a hole through Ernie, "I kill him. You understand that. I kill him when this is done. Tie him up!"

Norman pulls the tie wraps from his rear pants pocket and secures Ernie's hands to his belt in the back, and Demitre says, "OK, now do you want it here, or will you go to the vehicle without causing a fuss? It makes no difference to me."

Ernie, still cowering shifts his weight to try to get up and Henry kicks him back to the floor. Then Henry tells Ernie, "Speak puppy dog, speak."

Ernie replies, "OK, I'll go. If you let me," and he tries to get up again, this time watching Henry nervously. Henry backs out of his way, and after shifting his weight and spinning slightly, Ernie is able to get up on his own.

Demitre picks up his laptop and asks Ernie, "This? You were working with this?"

Norman jokes, "Hey, it's not the size of the tool, man."

Henry laughs, and the parade starts out of the apartment slowly. Guns put away, and no one paying any attention, Demitre says, "You live in a rat hole, Ernie, why do you even want to live?"

Ernie starts to grovel as they approach the SUV, with Malcolm in the rear passenger seat holding the door open, "I can be useful. You know I can. I can help. Hey, guys, I'm good with the computer."

Malcolm sneers and responds, "We don't care." Then talking to Henry, "Put him in the back with the trash."

They open the rear door of the SUV, and he crawls inside. One lady is watching from a window. Demitre sees her and holds up a fake badge, and she waves and pulls the curtain closed.

Demitre gets into the front passenger seat and asks Ernie, "Can you hear me, Ernie? How many friends do you have to come rescue you?" Henry puts a gag in Ernie's mouth and secures his feet and knees with tie wraps.

Ernie starts to whimper, and Norman, Henry and Bob laugh as Norman drives the SUV away from the apartment building.

Chapter 69

Norman is driving and Demitre is in the front passenger seat. They are now on Wilshire Boulevard, east bound off of the 405 Freeway. Demitre attempts to show on the screen of his smart phone a tiny picture of the top floor of the parking structure at the UCLA Medical Center. "This door," pointing, "is actually not set up for regular entry or exit from the hospital. Though it is used in emergency circumstances." The blueprints, suddenly scrolling electronically across Demitre's smart phone screen.

Demitre comments, "I wonder how many policemen will be stationed within five minutes of that parking structure now that you shot the place up?" After a breath, Demitre asks, "You had to shoot a doctor?"

Malcolm, flustered, answers, "I followed orders."

Demitre winks, "Exactly." The three men in the rear look at each other, hearing the ring of truth in Demitre's response. Henry, the farthest in the rear, looks down in the very back of the SUV, where Ernie is hogtied and now gagged looking up at the automatic weapon with real fear in his eyes. Ernie's eye is now swollen shut, and his breathing is slightly labored. Demitre says, "Remember, when we get there, I kill Uri and Ernie. You guys are backup. If it's the last thing I ever do I want to be the one to finish this."

Malcolm smiles from the side of his mouth away from Demitre, knowing that in fact, it will be the last thing he ever does. Finally, Malcolm asks, "What if all of those idiots show up?"

Demitre responds, "Then you have something to do. Can you handle that? If not, I need to know so I can get some more men."

Malcolm, already looking forward to ending his relationship with this Russian asshole, avoids the confrontation and says to his three men, "Do not interfere unless Mr. Demitre is incapable of finishing the task on his own. If he can't finish it by himself, kill him first." The three men glare at Demitre as Malcolm finishes, and Malcolm waits until the three nod back at him. Then he continues, "If there is trouble, Henry, seal the door. No re-entry to the hospital. Make sure if you cannot get up to block the door to make it a wasteland if anybody tries to get past. I will repeat this, we will exit through the hospital; there are thousands of exits. We meet at the Coffee Bean down the street. Clear?"

Henry looks at Malcolm and then back at Demitre and says, "Crystal."

At four o'clock, the Black Suburban pulls up to the mechanical kiosk to the parking area behind the UCLA Medical Center main building. Norman presses the red button, takes a time slip. Knowing that they will walk away from the parking structure when done, Norman discards the time slip and proceeds to the circular ramp leading to the top area. In the back, Henry points a silenced Beretta at Ernie's head and touches his fingers to his lips as they pass a doctor and a woman talking. The two completely ignore the large vehicle as it passes, and the men continue driving the circular ramp to the roof.

At the roof, Demitre points in an easterly direction and says, "Somewhere over there is the door." Norman, behind the wheel, defers to Malcolm, who nods his agreement, and the SUV goes in the direction pointed. To Malcolm, Demitre says, "I would park around the corner there," pointing around a corner of the parking area, "and then put your best shots there," pointing, "and there."

Malcolm says, "Do it," and they exit the vehicle. He adds, "Remember, you can't come back. Find your way out through the hospital in the chaos and we will meet down the street."

Ernie perks up and looks out the window as Henry turns away to watch the others find firing positions. Henry turns back and pops Ernie lightly on the head with the butt of his pistol. "Down doggy. Back in your hole." With fear and pain in his eyes, Ernie fights the gag in his mouth and holds back a tear. "If you're good, we'll give you a bone."

Malcolm, still in the passenger seat of the SUV, smiles. He looks at Demitre and asks, "Do you expect this to go the way you plan?"

Demitre smiles and responds knowingly, "You should know, Malcolm, nothing ever goes the way you plan it," and he winks at Malcolm as he hops out of the SUV and walks over to investigate the door.

Malcolm tells Henry, "Get out and stand behind the vehicle. Regardless of what Demitre wants, if your puppy dog back there moves or blinks, shoot him."

Henry nods and smiles wickedly at Ernie, "Be a good doggie and beg for Papa."

They get out, and Ernie is left alone for the first time since his capture. He is trapped, securely bound, and relying on the good intent of a man who has had already tried to kill him twice. A tear forms in his eye as he wallows in self-pity. Then Ernie starts to cry. He attempts but fails to spit out the gag, and he curls into a fetal ball in the back of the SUV.

Chapter 70

Haywood, seated in the waiting room of the hospital with Big Jim, asks Jim, "So do those boys ever stop eating?"

Big Jim smiles and changes the subject, "Did you know what was going to happen back at the post office?"

Haywood responds, "It could'a happened a hundred different ways, but we got lucky."

"Lucky is those six fools on the hillside. I was inside the restaurant eating pancakes when I heard the rumbling and thought, I hope by god that's thunder."

"Technology. We had the edge, and some dumb luck."

"You may believe that bullshit line, but I know better. I talked to Margaret and asked if I gave you my second in command in Rankin County, if she would move down with you." Haywood, stunned, just stares at the big man. Jim continues, "and she said she would come with you if you want."

A tear forms in the corner of Haywood's eye, and he responds, "So now you're some redneck matchmaker?"

"I just thought I could pay you what you're making as an investigator, and we could solve some crime together in hillbilly country."

Haywood retorts, "I suppose she worked out the

benefits package with you too?" Just then his phone rings, and he reaches to see Justin's number. "Justin, what's happening?"

"They are in position at the hospital pretty much right where you said they'd be, with Ernie in the back of the SUV."

"He's still alive; that was my biggest concern."

Justin adds, "Uri is going to be hanging out there if something goes wrong. Ernie can go screw himself. He picked his side."

"I'll watch Uri personally. Besides, Cardozo and Drescher posing as orderlies will be more in the line of fire than him. If it goes as planned, Malcolm and his men will see a show and go home convinced they are all dead."

Justin responds, "OK, you're the boss."

Haywood reminds him, "Remember to let us know if they move."

"OK."

As the clock ticks 4:30 PM, the rest of the group arrives and Haywood goes over the plan again. "Big Jim and you three," pointing at Albert, Evan and Robert, "stay out of view inside the door." Cardozo and Drescher are wearing body armor under loose-fitting orderly smocks. Cardozo, the swarthier of the two, is wearing glasses and a ball cap, and Drescher is wearing a wig and mustache. Both men have disheveled hair. Haywood continues, "Seeing you two, I just think it would be good if you didn't look around at them. I don't want them to get too good a view of you, OK?" They nod in the affirmative, and Haywood continues, "I'll drive the ambulance so they won't be able to see me. Demitre will walk over like he doesn't have a care and shoot us all dead, then walk away. If he aims at me first, I'll kill him right there and then. I told him that, and he knows why."

Evan asks, "OK, why?"

"Because if he aims at the only guy with a gun out, his intentions are bad. Good enough?"

Evan nods, "OK."

Haywood continues, "If anybody but Demitre comes out, I honk the horn and you two idiots," pointing at Cardozo and Drescher, "get the fuck out of the way. There are assault rifles in the back of the ambulance. I'll return fire and tell you what I see."

Albert asks, "Why no cops?"

Big Jim answers for him, "Because the bad guys will leave and Uri will still be alive. They might forget about you guys, but they've tried to kill Uri for the past ten years as far as I can see, and they will not stop unless they think he's a goner. Secondly, that's the deal we made with Demitre. If he holds up his end, we should be just fine."

Haywood asks them all, "Vests?" Everyone nods.

Chapter 71

Without belaboring coefficients of friction and the dynamics of ballistics, it is obvious that there is no safe place in a gunfight. Positions of safety, at least when bullets fly, are relative. Vests might block a bullet if it hits the vest. Even if it does hit the vest, the trauma can be so severe as to cause death anyway. The bullet may not pierce the flesh, but the impact is still massive. Then comes the math. Refraction, reflection and of course the true mystery of happenstance. How can a man three blocks away protect himself from a bullet traveling at X trajectory and Y speed that missed its primary target completely and is now destined for him? He can't see it. The sound will arrive after the bullet. He can only move to a neighborhood where gunfights don't happen.

The point is simply that there is no safe place in a gunfight. Ask Pat Tillman's family. The only safe way to have a gunfight is to not have a gun fight. As such, to knowingly delve into the realm of such stupidity means you have to harden yourself to the reality that you could die. That taken into consideration, if you have an option, you would want cold, experienced and unexcitable people with you.

Haywood realizes that his plan is fraught with risk. He pulls his worn red Washington Redskins cap down over his head and checks his resources. His faithful Berreta and the experimental Israeli rifle are at his side. He checks the fake mustache in the mirror, deciding it is about as good as it's going to look.

He fires the powerful engine in the ambulance and backs out onto the parking area. He pulls up to the parking kiosk and takes a ticket, pulls through and drives to the roof. Seeing the Suburban out of the corner of his eye, he feigns disinterest and pulls up toward the door. He executes a perfect thee-point turn and backs directly up to the door, leaving about fifteen feet for the action to take place and hopefully put this nightmare behind him.

Inside the door, Big Jim is in the front and Albert, Evan and Robert are directly behind as the gurney and the wheelchair roll toward the door. All are dressed in ill-fitting security uniforms with side arms and automatic rifles. The neck brace on the gurney hides a fact that would only be evident from directly overhead. The neck brace is shielding the face on a life sized dummy used in the hospital for training that is supporting a cheap wig similar in color to Barbara's hair. Albert looks back at the corner of the corridor where the girls wait, knowing that the real Barbara is still in the makeshift ICU set up in the secure area they selected.

Demitre checks his watch, and because Norman, Bob and Malcolm are all watching him out of the corner of their eyes, they knee jerk and check their watches too. Demitre sees the driver of the ambulance wearing a faded red baseball cap, and a glimpse of recognition causes him to smile briefly. He looks back at the others watching him and he checks his watch again. 4:55 PM. Five minutes to go. Suddenly, country music starts playing in the ambulance and Norman finds himself tapping his foot to the unfamiliar but simple beat. The song is an oldie, Conway Twitty's "Fifteen Years Ago Today."

Inside the ambulance, Haywood considers changing the channel but realizes suddenly that there might be a risk in that. If it's Haywood's ambulance, it would be Haywood's radio station, so leave it.

Big Jim turns his back to the door and says, "We only have surprise for a second because this door will be a killing zone. That means they will not allow anyone to go *in* this door. When we come out we need to do it at once and disburse quickly. So *please* find your own cover and get out of the door. There are probably no cars, and the pricks will be on both sides of the ambulance. Justin? Can you hear me?"

Justin responds, "Yep'er"

Robert jokes with his tongue out the side of his mouth, "Yep'er. Who says that?"

Big Jim continues, "Are they in the same places?"

Justin responds, "Why yes they are Mr. Big Jim , sir. Is that better asshole?"

Evan giggles under the tension from the silliness between the friends. There is a drawing of the parking area outside of the door taped to the wall. Referring to it, Big Jim concludes, "I'm going here," pointing to a location next to the ambulance. "I think both of you should get under the ambulance behind the tires. Albert, you're like me, too big to hide. I would suggest you stay in here."

Albert responds without thinking, "Not gonna happen."

They hear country music through the door and know Haywood is in location and ready. Cardozo says, "I really like that song."

Evan and Robert both gag, and Albert says, "You really are a shit-kicker, aren't you?"

Chapter 72

At exactly 5 pm, everyone tenses but nothing happens. The music continues, Ernie is frightened, Demitre tries to start a chain reaction by checking his watch. Still nothing happens. Suddenly they hear faint voices from behind the door which are muffled by the thickness of the door. Everyone tenses as the door rattles, and they hear Drescher yell, "Damn it."

Cardozo says, "Relax, here's the darn key."

After more clanking and rattling, the heavy door swings open and a wheel chair with Uri in it is wheeled out. Haywood leans back to the driver seat to be at the ready.

Next, comes Cardozo wheeling out the gurney with the dummy strapped safely on and asks, "Is this that Doctor?"

Drescher responds, "Yup, shot right downstairs, can you believe that?"

"No shit." Cardozo stops while Drescher opens the ambulance door. From the corner of everyone's eye, Demitre starts the expected walk toward the open door. Cardozo and Drescher act like they don't see him and go about their business. Drescher realizes that he has no idea at all as to how to get the wheelchair into the ambulance, so says, "Hey asshole, get up here and help me, would you.

You think I can do this on my own?"

Cardozo abandons the gurney and walks the few feet to the ambulance. Forgetting his instructions, he turns to Demitre and ad-libs, "What do you want?"

Close enough to act, Demitre pulls his pistol from his belt and shoots Oscar in the plastic head then turns and shoots Uri in the back of his head as Uri pulls a pistol from his lap. Uri falls forward out of the chair partly under the ambulance, out of the way. Haywood pulls his cap off and Malcolm yells to Demitre, "The driver, the driver!" as the two men exchange fire and blood splatters against the windshield.

Demitre spins around and shoots both orderlies and pulls out his clip to replace it. He slides it into his pistol and says, "How did you know?"

Before he can tell him, Malcolm hears a yell from behind, "Everybody freeze!" A security guard standing next to the stair well entrance with his pistol drawn and aimed at Henry, still standing in front of the SUV.

Demitre walks directly toward the SUV as Henry looks to Malcolm. Malcolm pivots and shoots the security guard through the head. He falls backward in slow motion as Demitre opens the rear door to the SUV and shoots Ernie three times.

With everyone's attention directed at the SUV, Robert and Evan run out of the hospital door in the ill-fitting security uniforms, assume there positions under the ambulance as Big Jim yells, "Security, drop the guns!"

As the four turn back toward the door, Demitre shoots Henry and a shot comes from the ambulance dropping Demitre with a surprised look on his face, blood oozing from under his shirt, pooling freely on his back. Norman and Bob fall immediately from a volley coming from the ground area behind the ambulance tires, and a ricochet of debris off of a concrete wall cuts Malcolm's ear severely. Daubing his ear with his sleeve, Malcolm flinches from the pain and runs past the fallen security guard for the stairwell. Without pausing, Malcolm looks briefly over his shoulder to confirm that all of his men are down and presumed dead. At the stairwell, with no hesitation, he runs down five flights of stairs two steps at a time.

At the bottom of the stairs, still daubing his ear, he picks a random direction, knowing he has no one left to "meet up" with. He immediately starts looking for a car to commandeer. He slows down to watch as a truck driver in a delivery van stops and gets out with a package, leaving the engine still running. Malcolm walks over to make sure the driver is not coming right back out and hops into the back of the van.

In the back, he strips off his clothes and wraps his ear with Kleenex from a box on a shelf. As the driver gets in, Malcolm puts the still warm pistol against his ear and says,

"Get in the back and take off your clothes."

As quickly as possible, the man takes off his clothing. Malcolm puts on the large clothing and secures the driver's hands with wrapping tape from a small supply shelf. Malcolm lies, "Sit down and relax and you'll live through this."

Orienting himself in the medium-sized van, he engages the gearshift and pulls slowly away from the curb.

Chapter 73

With his gun drawn in the echoing aftermath of the assault, Haywood inches toward the three bodies and removes the earplugs with one hand and puts them in his pocket. As he clears the side of the ambulance, the others stir and start moving forward. Still with his gun moving toward anything that moved, he sees Demitre stand and keeps his aim firmly on him. Demitre says, "I thought I was good now."

Haywood responds as he frisks Demitre and wipes the fake blood on his pants "That doesn't mean that I trust you. Ernie? You OK?"

Ernie responds, "Yeah, scared shitless, but OK."

Haywood says, "When your buddy shot that asshole over there, I wasn't sure if you were still alive."

Demitre smiles and responds, "Three blanks for Ernie, then I'm hot. It is after all, a gunfight where I'm supposed to be a victim."

Haywood nods and then looks at them and says, "You have one hour and then I set the dogs on you if I ever hear your name again, you got that?"

Demitre starts walking back toward the door to the hospital as Ernie asks, "We did what you wanted. Why the hard act?"

Haywood responds, "Because you worked for the bad guys. That makes you a bag guy. You got a guy killed and put my friends in danger. Now get the hell out of here before I have to explain who you are to the cops!"

So Ernie runs to catch up with Demitre and asks him, "Are we good? I let you shoot me?"

"Don't think you can use me for a reference. But I'm done killing."

Everyone leaves the area except Haywood, despite protestations from Big Jim and the others. Haywood sits on the ground and waits, as the first team of badges, run up the stairwell, and look around in disbelief. Haywood, with his arms raised passively over his head, yells to the officers, "Over here. Hey, over here!"

One officer asks, "You OK?"

Haywood responds, "Not emotionally I'm afraid."

The other officer looks around and asks, "What the hell happened?"

Haywood says, hearing several sirens in the background, "Lets wait for the rest so I don't have to explain too many times."

The security patrolmen are somewhat confused by the response. One maintains a bead on Haywood and the other looks around at the chaos. "Holy shit! What's the dummy doing here with a wig on?"

The remaining evidence consists of a gurney and ambulance with corn syrup colored with red die number 2, three dead guys shot from weapons that are nowhere to be found, one dead security guard shot by one of the guns found and a pool of the same corn syrup combination beside an SUV.

Downstairs in the waiting room, Big Jim is wringing his hands in concern for his friend as Albert walks up and says, "He'll be OK."

Big Jim smiles and says, "I can't be having my new second in command doing two to ten in prison, is all."

Albert smiles, "Is he going to go work for you?"

Big Jim responds, "I can't have my friends working for the likes of you morons." This comment elicits a chuckle from the other friends in the room. "He should be OK. But you know how things can go. Three dead guys are unknown commodities. It's horrible that the security guard showed up. Don't tell Barbara till she's better, OK? As for Haywood, the fact that he had a gun with blanks and waited when he could have run will go a long way for his credibility. That drug thing is, well, another unknown. I'd say a toss up. Sixty-forty he walks away."

Up in the parking area the detectives have arrived and Haywood has given them McHugh's telephone number. As one detective waits for the call to go through, Haywood offers to the other, "This is my gun, I was shooting blanks."

The cop looks at him confused, "You went to a gun fight with a load of blanks."

"There wasn't supposed to be a gun fight, now was there."

Still confused, the detective asks, "OK, then what the hell happened?"

"I'm a retired FBI agent, he's calling my boss," pointing to the other detective on the phone now talking to someone, "I was just trying to stay out of the way when all hell broke loose."

The other detective hands Haywood his phone, "He asked for you."

As Haywood starts to say hello, McHugh ask's, "What in the holly hell is going on?"

Haywood smiles and responds while the detectives are listening, "The guys that were trying to steal the missiles got into a gun fight when we were trying to decoy a target they were after. A doctor who saw one of their faces and got shot at UCLA yesterday--I was just trying to protect her. You said I wasn't supposed to carry a gun, so I got a blank gun at a movie supply store. The thing went to hell when someone else got involved and took three of four out. The leader, named Malcolm, probably South African, size and weight unknown, seems to have gotten away. I'll bet these dead guys turn out to be from the same place."

McHugh says, "You are an idiot, have I ever said that?"

Haywood responds, "Yes sir."

"Could you let me talk to the detectives please?" Haywood hands the phone back to the detective.

"Yes sir?"

Listening, the detectives says again, "Yes sir." He looks at Haywood sideways and then, "Yes sir, I would be happy to."

Haywood, ready for anything, waits as the detectives walk away and talk. One goes toward the door, and the other comes back to Haywood. He tells Haywood, "He said you were a bit crazy but a good cop. He also said if you wanted a favor, it would be OK with him if we did it. What would that be?"

Haywood smiles at the unspoken connection he had made with his ex-boss and says simply, "I would like to be dead."

"What?"

Chapter 74

On the 405 Freeway north, with a deliriously frightened driver now gagged and bound in the back, Malcolm approaches an off ramp. He gets off the freeway at Ventura Boulevard and pulls into the Galleria parking structure. Malcolm looks up at the last minute and flinches, concerned about overhead clearance. As he clears the eleven-foot marker, he sighs and pulls out of the way. He checks the mirror to see his shredded ear and does what he can before getting out of the van. Once he is out of view of the driver and anyone else, he puts the suppressor from his pocket onto his pistol. Then he opens the van. door and fires a single round into the frightened man's forehead. Instead of leaving, Malcolm walks farther into the parking area and finds a fifteen-year-old Ford. He reaches into his pocket and takes out a pre-bent thin strip of metal and jimmies the door open.

As the alarm goes off, he looks around and sits in the driver seat, after a beat he disables the alarm and starts the car. As he leaves the parking structure, he dials his phone. He gets back on the 405 freeway south and waits for the ring.

The ringing phone wakes Carl. He clearly does not like to be disturbed during his limited sleeping time. However, he knows that the call is coming, so he reaches with some trepidation for the phone and says, "Oui?"

Trapped in bumper-to-bumper traffic on his way to the airport, Malcolm struggles forward at 10 miles per hour and says, "They are all dead; Uri, Haywood, and the doctor. The big kaffer is dead or injured or he would have been there when his wife died."

Carl relaxes, "That may be the best we can hope for. How about your men?"

"Dead."

Carls softens, "I am so sorry. Are you going home?"

Malcolm gets a sudden flash of reality. Remembering how Carl has been dealing with ex-employees, he responds, "Not unless you need me there. I was going to drive down to Mazatlan to see an old girlfriend. I don't have anything to go back to."

Carl notes the concern in Malcolm's voice and asks, "Could you put another team together in a week or two? Take some time off."

"A week, maybe 10 days."

Carl signs off saying, "Then I'll call back in a week." Malcolm opens the back of his phone, takes out the battery and sim card and tosses them out the window.

Haywood walks into the hospital room where Barbara is surrounded by the entire gang, except Uri. Haywood says to Barbara, "God you look good!" Margaret immediately comes around the bed to meet her husband, and Albert fakes a growl.

Barbara weakly jokes, "Watch out, I'm married to a jealous man."

The group hug stops, when Big Jim asks, "So what do the cops say?"

Haywood sighs and starts, "They have no idea what they're looking for. The guys that are going to be blamed for the attempt at the missiles are dead in the parking lot, except for a guy named Malcolm who nobody can swear to what he looks like. I saw him from 50 feet behind an automatic weapon, so to me he looked like a gun barrel. Tomorrow the newspapers are going to say that I died in the crossfire without a weapon on me.

Albert suggests, "It occurs to me that it's not going to help your investigation business, being dead, I mean."

Haywood looks down and then backup at Big Jim, "I get to go back to what I do best, be a cop."

Margaret adds, "A married cop?"

Chapter 75

The explosive charges have been set, Demitre drives into the Riverside County Public Utilities Company parking area and turns off his lights. In the dark of midnight, he walks casually across to the gate area and punches in a code. The heavy gate rolls easily out of the way. He walks over to a clearly marked county van and pops the hood. He takes the spare key from its not-so-secret hiding place and climbs into the distinctively marked van. He puts on the County of Riverside shirt, starts the engine and drives out the gate. He stops to close the gate behind him and then drives the two and a half blocks to the Riverside Courthouse. There he parks near the wall closest to the holding cells. The holding cells are considered by most to be the highest security containment center in Riverside County.

Checking his watch as the seconds tick off, he counts down in Russian, "Tree, dva, a-deen." An explosion is heard in the distance. He pulls out his cell phone and sees that he has no cellular reception at all. He smiles. He gets out of the big van and crouches behind it in the shadows, and another explosion happens and then a third, and every light as far as the eye can see blinks out. Then there is dead silence. The silence is broken by the sound of a dog barking and a collision can be heard in the distance. Demitre makes a note to drive extra safe until the lights go back on.

Suddenly, the wall on the building a hundred feet away explodes and collapses away from the building. Demitre walks casually over to the fallen wall as his six comrades captured in Pioneertown, now in orange coveralls, walk out the hole. They are dragging a man in a guard uniform out into the darkness. Demitre whispers as loud as he dare, "Toropit'sya."

The men turn to the voice and run toward him. Pavel points to the guard, and Demitre says, "Bring him." They all pile into the utility van, and Demitre turns on his emergency light and drives to the 15 freeway west.

At Corona, he pulls off the freeway, pulls up next to a 10-passenger tour bus and stops. The seven men all get out of the van and Ernie opens the door to the tour bus. and the men in orange coveralls all climb aboard. After he checks the guard, now safely bundled and gaged in the van, Demitre reaches out his hand to Ernie and says, "You do have skills."

Ernie responds, "But I need top-of-the-line gear."

Demitre looks back at the nervous group and says, "And you shall have it. Let's go."

South on the 15 they turn toward the Otay Mesa

Crossing a few miles out of the way and get completely across the boarder before they hear the first radio broadcast about the escape from the Riverside Jail. The radio announces that the authorities know little but believe the escapees are still in the immediate area.

The grateful men are gathered around a large table at Breakfast in Ensenada, Mexico, at La Corazon Hotel on the Marina. They are listing to a young woman sing in a lyrical voice, accompanied by a harp in the corner. As she takes a break, Demitre leans forward and says, "My friends, comrades, what I, we," pointing to Ernie, "have done, we did for honor. For that, you owe us nothing. We are unemployed, and I am now dead," he smiles and there are a few chuckles around the table, "so I have no promise of work, though we do have a certain reserve available. Since we have certain resources," again pointing at Ernie, "available to us, I do have an offer. No obligation, as I know several of you have families. But we would like to start our own business, and you will be my bosses."

The men look at each other, unsure of the meaning exactly, so Demitre continues, "They have Columbians here, Arabs, Mexicans and Salvadorans. So why not Russians? We have enough capital to set up where-ever we want. I propose we start out own cartel."

www.ingramcontent.com/pod-product-compliance
Lightning Source LLC
Chambersburg PA
CBHW071243170626
46809CB00001B/78